On the cover, a hand made of sheet mica from the indigenous American people known in this era as the Hopewell Culture. The hand (C. 100 B.C.) was found in a burial mound in the Ohio Valley. Since mica is too fragile for any practical use, anthropologists suggest that these delicate pieces were created as burial gifts, to accompany the dead into the next world.

The Hopewell Culture was part of a larger cultural group, the Woodland Indians. These people lived in small tribes throughout what is now the eastern half of the United States and all through Canada and Alaska. Their ancestors were Asian immigrants who crossed the Bering Straits onto the American continent.

Many of the images and symbols of the Woodland Indians bear a striking resemblance to those of early Vedic culture in India, including interlaced pairs of snakes, whirling swastika designs, two-faced personages and figures meditating in the lotus posture.

In Vedic tradition, stretching further back than anyone can remember, beyond the western sense of time and history and into mythic time, the right hand held up and open means "fear not." In Hindu and Buddhist practice, it is the abhāya mudra.

Fire Over Water

Edited by Reese Williams

TANAM PRESS 1986

For Elizabeth Enchin

Reese Will

11/12/86

TANAM PRESS
40 WHITE STREET
NEW YORK, NY 10013

TANAM PRESS GRATEFULLY ACKNOWLEDGES SUPPORT
FROM THE NEW YORK STATE COUNCIL ON THE ARTS
LITERATURE PROGRAM

Cover photo courtesy of the Field Museum of Natural History,
Chicago.

IN MEMORY OF THERESA HAK KYUNG CHA

Contents

Preface

"Fire over water" is the image of the 64th hexagram of the *I Ching,* *Before Completion.*

THE IMAGE

Fire over water:
The image of the condition before transition.
Thus the superior man is careful
In the differentiation of things,
So that each finds its place.

I had approached the *I Ching* seeking guidance on how to cnd my work with Tanam Press. "So that each finds its place" was the line that stayed with me in the days that followed. I remembered my first impulse to publish which took form as *Hotel* (Tanam Press, 1980). This book, a collection with seven contributors, was not "edited" in the usual sense of the word. Instead of selecting work that I felt merited greater attention, I invited seven people to create new work for *Hotel.* It was understood that we would go with whatever they came up with, and that their "being together" would be the book.

I'm sure there are precedents in publishing history for this type of book, but if I trace my editorial sensibility to its source, I find myself in art classes with Jim Melchert at U. C. Berkeley in the mid 1970s. In

1

these classes we worked on assignments collaboratively in small groups and then reported back to the larger group of the class. Each group (they changed from day to day) had its own particular energy— sometimes delightful, sometimes frustrating. Looking back, I realize that we were learning to find our selves, to "find our place" in relation to the group dynamic, not in relation to our teacher's practice of art or to conceptions of art that were circulating in the culture at the time. It was an incredibly free place, there was no right or wrong. Value was placed on experimentation, change and surprise, not so much on outcome or end product.

About a week after receiving the "Fire over water" image, I knew that I needed to edit and publish one more book for Tanam Press. I envisioned the book quickly, within the space of one hour; I "saw" how it looked—the cover, the design—and knew who the contributors would be and in what sequence their work would appear. As with *Hotel*, people were asked to create or choose work for this occasion. But unlike *Hotel* which was all short fiction, *Fire Over Water* is a wide-ranging collection of poetry, prose and critical essays. Without knowing what the contributors would do, I knew that bringing this group of people into the space of one book would articulate the synthesis that I had been attempting with Tanam Press more clearly than ever before, thus allowing the press to "find its place."

At the time of this writing, I have had all the manuscripts for three weeks, and the interrelationships, sub-themes and synchronicities are beginning to come forward. A constellation of ten points, this book stands as a sign, a sign representing the sense of place that is created whenever diverse forces come together inspired by the desire to (re)establish connection.

With a *thank you* and a bow to each of the contributors, I welcome you into this book.

R.W.

Fire Over Water

Cecilia Vicuña

Palabrarmás

Translated by Eliot Weinberger

Open your mouth and receive the host of the wounded word

Vicente Huidobro

THE ORIGINAL BOOK *Palabrarmás* was born from a vision in which individual words opened to reveal their inner associations, allowing ancient and newborn metaphors to come to light.

In 1966 nearly a hundred of these words appeared. I called them *divinations*, and ceased to think much about them.

Then in 1974, they appeared again, arming themselves with a name, *palabrarmás* (*palabra*, word; *labrar*, to work; *armas*, arms; *maś*, more). A word that means: to work words as one works the land is to work more; to think of what the work does is to arm yourself with the vision of words. And more: words are weapons, perhaps the only acceptable weapons. That same year I began to find ancient and modern texts which helped me to understand what I had seen.

I now think of this way of seeing words as a nuclear vision: any place we choose to enter its nucleus or heart will lead to a point of revelation.

Palabrarmás, published in Buenos Aires in 1984, may be impossible to translate in its entirety. The book is in five parts. The first three—the poem, the divinations, and *palabrarmás*—contain the vision. Each opened word leads to another, and the metaphoric suggestions are mainly applicable to Spanish. But the last two parts—*to open words* and *to coincide*—meditations on the consequences of the previous sections, can indeed be translated.

The following text is a condensed version of that meditation. The notes include some of the texts which served as a kind of mirror or confirmation of the original intuitions.

9

I

To approach words from poetry is a form of asking questions.

To ask questions is to fathom, to drop a hook to the bottom of the sea.

The first questions appeared as a vision: I saw in the air words that contained, at the same time, both a question and an answer.

I called them divinations. And the words said: the word *is* the divination; to divine is to ascertain the divine.

Other numerical and calendrical systems speak of what has come or what will come, but only the word is the divination of what we are now and why.

"Think of the constellations, they too are forms"

Piet Mondrian

In Spanish, *preguntar, to ask*, from the Latin *percontari*, from *contus*, hook.

The insistence on *seeing* words, in their double sense, interior and exterior, is universal. (To write and to read are also ways of seeing.)

"I don't see with my eyes: words
are my eyes"

Octavio Paz, A Draft of Shadows.

In Nahuatl, the ancient language of Central Mexico, the sage was called *tlamatini*, "the one who knows something," described in poetry as:

> "Those who see
> who dedicate themselves to observing
> the course and ordered ways of heaven
> how is night divided.
> Those who are watching (reading)
>
> They carry us, they guide us
> they tell us the way"

Libro de los coloquios, transcribed
by Fray Bernardino de Sahagún.

To see, from the Indo-European root *wid*, Germanic *wit*, Old English wise, wit, knowledge. Latin *videre*, view, vision. Suffixed form *wid-es-ya* in Greek *idea*, appearance, form. In Sánskrit *veda*, knowledge and "I have seen."

To divine, from the Indo-European root *da, dai* in Greek *daiesthai*, to divide. Suffixed form *dai-mon*, divider, provider, divinity.

A word is divine: internally divided.
Its inner division creates its ambiguity, the inner tension that makes growth and association possible. Division that can be expressed in multiple ways: —putting two parts together, as in root + suffix. —com-pounding, putting two words into one. —putting two antithetical meanings in one.
(Freud sees the latter one still being expressed in the dream's work, where a thing can mean its opposite.)

Ambiguous, from the Latin *ambigere, ambi*, around + *agere*, to drive, lead. To lead around. (Later on (?) *ambi* comes to mean *both*. In Spanish *ambiguous* is "that which is discussed," divided.

11

Words want to speak; to listen to them is the first task.

To open words is to open oneself.

To discover the ancient metaphors condensed in the word itself.

A history of words would be a history of being, but this writing is only a meditation through hints and fragments—from the imagination, for the imagination.

imagen en acción   image in action

"Mortals speak insofar as they listen."
"This speaking that listens and accepts is responding."
Martin Heidegger, *Poetry, Language and Thought*

Abrir, to open in Spanish, from the Latin *aperire*, from *parere*, to give birth, to separate in two parts as in opening a clam shell.

"Name; the word seems to be a compressed sentence, signifying being for which there is a search."

Plato, *Cratylus*

"To discuss language, to place it, means to bring to its place of being not so much language as ourselves: our own gathering into the appropriation."

Heidegger, *Ibid.*

"Those who do not bring together the permanent togetherness hear but resemble the deaf."

Heraclitus, *Fragment 34*

"The whole delicate substance of speech is built upon substrate of metaphor. Abstract terms, pressed by etymology, reveal their ancient roots still embedded in direct action."
Ernest Fenollosa, *The Chinese Written Character as a Medium for Poetry.*

"The first imposers of names were philosophers."

Plato, *Cratylus*

Words contain in their own ambiguity, both the division of language and its potential unity.

All cultures have been aware of this division of language, whether it is in two or more kinds of words, or in two or more uses: the sacred and the profane.

"According to Bhartrihari, two kinds of language exist. One is made from word-seeds *(sphota)*, ideas inalterables, that are modulations of the universal *atman*, the real divisions of the universe. (*Sphota* evokes the blossoming of a flower, the development of a bud—thus a constant germinative power hidden beneath the appearances which manifest it.) The other kind is created from sonorous words *(dhvani)*, usual words, subordinated to natural laws, that is to the rules of phonetics and grammar."

Rene Daumal, *Rasa*

(Bhartrihari, fifth century A.D.? An adept of the *Vedanta*, he expounded its linguistic doctrine in the *Vakyapadiya* "Of the Phrase and the Word.")

13

Words take us, mark us, they contain within the ideas that keep us moving.

Every people is its language, the vision they inherit.
To create is to set out from the first images, the original pattern.

But throughout history words have concealed and revealed, constantly transforming.

Having lost the memory of the original meaning, we can invent an *etymon* (true meaning), one that contains within what the word will be. To go backward and inward simultaneously. To contemplate the origins and the future. The ancient and current signified.

revelar	to reveal
volver a velar	to re-veil

considerar el origen	To consider the origin
es con y sideralmente	is to con(template)side(really)
contemplar el *oriri;*	study together the *oriri:*
salir de los astros	the coming out of the stars

To enter words in order to see, is the point of word-working: to work speech, to speak watching speech work.

To split the word *word*—and *metaphor* and *poetry:*

"Since being means emerging, appearing, to issue forth from concealment, its origin in concealment belongs to it essentially."

Martin Heidegger, *Introduction to Metaphysics*

"Being inclines intrinsically to self concealment."

Heraclitus, *Fragment 123 (Ibid.)*

"In the didactic texts, the Vedic glossaries, the commentaries to the
sacred works, still another resource of language is employed. It is the
nirukta, 'explication of words,G'" . . . *nirukta* does not presume to be a
scientific 'etymology'—if indeed a scientific etymology could exist. The
nirukta 'explains' a word by developing the meanings contained in its
constituent parts and the verbal associations that could help the memory to retain its content and the diverse aspects of the idea that it signifies . . . the explication of *saman* 'liturgical chant,' from *sa* (she) + *ama*
(he), developed at length in the *Chandogya Upanishad,* reminds the poet
that by chanting he activates within himself a marriage between two
forces, male and female; and elsewhere, the same text gives for the
same word, a totally different explanation,. . . This digression seemed
necessary to underline the *spiritually practical* (and not intellectually
discursive) value of the Hindu verbal elaborations."

(First published in *Les Cahiers du Sud,* No. 236, 1941. Later reprinted in
Les Pouvoirs de la Parole, Paris: Gallimard, 1970. English version by
Louise Landes Levi, in *Rasa* by Rene Daumal, New Directions, 1982.)

The word compares, puts side by side what is known and what is to be known.

To work words is to be with, to con-verse—what the word says about being is what we will know.

> con o cer   to know:
>
> ser con   to be with

The word works parabolically, and its work, above all, re-works the wordworker.

palabra es pala y abra   Word is a shovel, an opening
para que entre la luz   for light to come in

The word is articulated silence and sound, organized light and shadow.

It crisscrosses and combines forms of energy, it lets sound see, the image hear.

Air or modulated breath, it simultaneously constructs and destructs.

The double nature, the essential ambiguity that is the source of asking questions.

The word creates the being, or is created by it, in a mystery of which we only have the keys to make it grow.

16

Comparar, to compare: to stand beside.

"Our concepts owe their existence to comparisons"

Sigmund Freud

"Something is present to us. It stands steadily by itself and thus manifests itself. It is. For the Greeks "being" basically meant this standing presence."

". . .standing in itself was nothing other than standing there, standing in the light."

"The original emergence and standing of energies, the *phainesthai,* or appearance in the great sense of the word epiphany, becomes a visibility of things that are already there and can be pointed out."

"*Logos* means the word, discourse, and *legein* means to speak, as in dia-logue, mono-logue. But originally *logos* did not mean speech, discourse . . . *Lego, legein,* Latin *legere,* is the same as the German word "lesen": to gather, to collect, read . . . which is: to put one thing with another, to bring together, in short, to gather."

Martin Heidegger, *Introduction to Metaphysics*

Heraclitus, *Fragment 1*: "But while the *logos* remains always this, men remain uncomprehending, both before they have heard and just after they have heard. For everything becomes essent in accordance with this *logos*. . ."
Fragment 2: "Therefore it is necessary to follow it, i.e. to adhere to togetherness in the essent; but though the *logos* is this togetherness in the essent, the many live as though each had his own understanding (opinion)." (Ibid.)

In the Nahuatl language, the creator or giver of life is invoked with the name *"Tloque Nahuaque,"* literally: "the owner of togetherness and nearness."

Miguel León Portilla, *The Ancient Mexicans*

17

Metaphor, from the Greek *meta-*
phora, from *metapherein,* to carry
or transfer. *Meta:* beyond.
Pherein: to carry.

Joan Corominas

The metaphor carries beyond, toward the most complex and
the most specific forms of comparison; to the furthest, the
limits of knowledge, to the essence, the heart of being, to its
reason for being.

co n razón   heart with reason

An essence dependent on the parabola that tracks it and cannot be named other than by analogy or suggestion.

The metaphor carries beyond for love.

It searches for, desires the union of name and named.

"In Nahuatl the artist is *tlayolteuanni*, he who sees with his heart."
Eliot Weinberger, *Octavio Paz Collected Poems*

"*Heart, yóllotl*, in Nahuatl is derived etymologically from the root *oll-in*, 'movement,' which in its abstract form *yóll-otl* signifies the idea of 'mobility,' the mobility of each one."

". . .In describing the supreme ideal of Nahua men and women, they say that they must be 'owners of a face, owners of a heart.'" ". . .the supreme ideal of education, *Ixtlamachiliztli*, is the 'action of giving wisdom to the faces,' . . . and *Yolmelahualiztli*, 'the action of straightening the heart.'"
Miguel León Portilla, *The Ancient Mexicans*

In the Popol Vuh, Maya Quiche, "God" is the "Heart of Heaven."

"Anything which moves, is moved because of something which it does not have, which thereby constitutes the end of its motion."
Dante Alighieri, *The Letter to Can Grande.*

In the Hindu poetics, "a poem is recognized as such by 'those who have a heart.'"
Rene Daumal, *Ibid.*

> "Who impels us to utter these words?
> What cannot be spoken with words,
> but that whereby words are spoken."
> *Kena Upanishad*

One metaphor carries another within it; only poetry can guarantee the continuance of the species.

A rising toward the precision where the metaphor reaches terrains of splendor.

Splendor *is* creation.

A union of disparate forces, the word condenses creation within its inner metaphors.

Metaphors carry beyond, opening (giving birth to) new worlds for the imagination.

"Sacred knowledge and, by extension, wisdom are conceived as the fruit of an initiation, and it is significant that obstetric symbolism is found connected with the awakening of consciousness both in ancient India and in Greece. Socrates had good reason to compare himself to a midwife, for in fact he helped men to be born to consciousness of the self . . . The Buddha, . . . 'engendered' by his 'mouth,' that is, by imparting his doctrine *(dhamma)*.
Mircea Eliade, *The Sacred and the Profane*

The Indo-European root *bher*, to carry, also to bear children. (Latin *ferre*, to carry, confer, differ, fertile, suffer), Greek *pherein*, to carry, amphora, euphoria, metaphor.

And *nomn-bher*, "to bear a name."

Poetry, from the Greek *poiesis*,
creation, from *poiein:* to make.
Joan Corominas

Poetry condenses the desire of words to create through union and multiplication.

The work of metaphor-making.

Words have a love for each other, a desire that culminates in poetry,

Union of man and his word, word with word.

For love we make words, not for necessity—for love is the only necessity.

ver dad	truth:
dar ver	to give sight
verdadera	truthful:
es dadora de ver	giver of sight
ver el sentido del dar	to see the meaning of giving
es el trabajo del palabrar	is the work of words

The word's desire to be, to grow and spread seems to be part of its being, as being means appearing, and desire means to shine.

"Be is from *bhu*, to grow."

Fenollosa, Ibid.

Desire, from the Latin *desiderare*, to long for, formed in analogy with *considerare*, "to observe the stars carefully." *Sidus*, star, constellation: sidereal, from the Indo-European root *sweid*: to shine.

In a time when stars are sacred, and their contemplation is a sacred activity, the desire for their shining, is the desire for god.

". . .the word for 'god,' *deiw-os*, and the two-word name of the chief deity of the pantheon *dyeu-pater* (Latin Jupiter, Greek Zeus, Sánskrit Dyaus pitar. . .) [are] derivatives of a root *deiw*, meaning to 'shine.'"

Calvert Watkins

"And so the author says well when he writes that the divine ray, or divine glory, 'penetrates through the universe and shines,' for it penetrates, as the beginning of essence, and shines, as the beginning of being."

Dante Alighieri, quoting Aristotle's Physics. The Letter to Can Grande

". . .He wished him to speak, that in the manifestation of so great a gift He might be glorified. . ."

Dante Alighieri, De Vulgari Eloquentia.

To grow and *to create* are associated from the beginning as well; both are derived from the root form *ker*, suffixed form *ker-es*, in Latin Ceres, goddess of agriculture (cereal), and the Latin *creare*, from the suffixed form *kre-ya*.

"The nature of poetry, in turn, is the founding of truth."
". . .founding in the triple sense of bestowing, grounding, and beginning."

Martin Heidegger, Poetry, Language, Thought.

"*Truth*, in Náhuatl, *neltiliztli*, is a term derived from the same root as *tla-nélhuatl*, which in turn is directly derived from *nelhuáyotl*: foundation."
". . .etymologically *truth* for the Nahuas was in its abstract form (*neltiliztli*), the quality of standing firmly, of being well grounded, of having good foundations."

Miguel León Portilla, Ibid.

Truth, in English, is derived from the Indo-European root *deru*, to be firm, solid, steadfast. Suffixed form variant *drew-o* in Germanic *trewan*, in Old English *treow*, tree.

23

The word is the point of confluence and union, the ray in prayer.

A minimal, an essential poem, the word *is* poetry; to speak is to pray.

Flower is the word flower
Joao Cabral de Melo Neto

The word has been created by and for poetry, and with poetry we give thanks for the grace we have received, life.

"Un-concealment occurs only when it is achieved by work: the work of the word in poetry. . ."
"work is to be taken here in the Greek sense of *ergon*, the creation that discloses the truth."

Martin Heidegger, Introduction to Metaphysics

Oración in Spanish is speech and prayer at the same time. From the Latin *orare*, to speak and pray.

"Prayer is perfect when he who prays remembers not that he is praying."

Anonymous, The Upanishads, translation by Juan Mascaró

"What then did the voice of the first speaker say? I have no hesitation in saying that it must at once be clear to any man of sound mind that it was the word for 'God,' that is *El*, either as a question or as an answer."

Dante Alighieri, De Vulgari Eloquentia

"Thus in all poetry a word is like a sun"

Fenollosa, Ibid.

"Poetry is a word whose essence is savor." (Sahitya Darpana)
"Savor" (rasa) is knowledge, "shining in itself."

Rene Daumal, Ibid.

"Glory is in Greek *doxa*. *Dokeo* means: I show myself, appear, enter into the light."

". . .For Pindar to glorify was the essence of poetry and the work of the poet was to place in the light."

". . .for the Greeks standing-in-itself was nothing other than standing there, standing-in-the-light. Being means appearing."

Martin Heidegger, Introduction to Metaphysics

II

In the Mbyá Guaraní creation myth, love, language and sacred song
are created all at once:

Appearing [in human form]
from the wisdom inside his own light
and by virtue of this creator wisdom
he conceived the origin of human language

Having conceived the origin of the future
human language
from the wisdom inside his own light
and by virtue of this creator wisdom
he conceived the idea of love [in union with the other]

Having created the idea of human language
having created a small sliver of love
from the wisdom inside his own light
and by virtue of this creator or wisdom
he created in his loneliness
the seed of a single sacred song

And then
from the wisdom inside his own light
and by virtue of this creator wisdom
he imparted
to the true father of the future Karai
to the true father of the future Tupa
knowledge of this light
To make true fathers of the word-souls
of their many future children
he imparted knowledge of this light

> from La Literatura de los Guaraníes,
> León Cadogán. Translated from the
> Spanish by David Guss.

"There was nothing standing; only the calm water, the placid sea, alone and tranquil. Nothing existed.
There was only immobility and silence in the darkness, in the night. Only the Creator, the Maker, Tepeu, Gucumatz, the Forefathers, were in the water surrounded with light. They were hidden under green and blue feathers, and were therefore called Quetzal Serpent. By nature they were great sages and great thinkers. In this manner the sky existed and also the Heart of Heaven, which is the name of God and thus He is called.

26

So then came his word here.
　　It reached
To Majesty
　　and Quetzal Serpent
There in the obscurity,
　　In the nightime.
It spoke to Majesty
　　And Quetzal Serpent, and they spoke.
Then they thought;
　　Then they pondered.
Then they found themselves;
　　They assembled
Their words,
　　Their thoughts.
Then they gave birth—
　　Then they heartened themselves.

> The Popol Vuh Maya Quiché
> Translations by Delia Goetz &
> Sylvanus Morley (prose) and by
> Munro Edmonson (verse)

"OM. This eternal Word is all: what was, what is and what shall be, and what beyond is in eternity. All is OM."

> *Mandukya Upanishad*
> Translation by Juan Mascaró

"In the beginning was the Word, and the Word was with God; and the Word was God."

> Saint John

". . .by the fire of fervour arose the ONE. And in the ONE arose love. Love the first seed of the soul."

> *Rig Veda* X,129

"Language falls, comes from above as little luminous objects that fall from heaven, which I catch word after word with my hands."

> María Sabina

"The word sign is radical supposedly from combination of tongue and above: ?."

> Ernest Fenollosa

"O fellow poets, we must take it upon ourselves
To stand, heads bared, beneath the tempests
Of the Lord, and seize the Father's lightning

27

With our hands, and offer the people
This gift of heaven, veiled in song."

Friedrich Hölderlin
Translation by Richard Sieburth

The common ground shared by these and so many other texts—what does it say? That we are all thinking together, but expressing ourselves in thousands of ways that are both different and the same? Or that an ancient wisdom, suppressed and forgotten, is revived in the poetic thought of every era?

To approach the one verse, the word as a uni-verse, is a universal phenomenon.

To communicate is to listen.

comun unica acción   communication: common action

Communication contains the potential for common action.

What doors would listening together open?

From time immemorial, the word has wanted to speak. From the text *In the beginning was the Word. . .* and from our having been *created in His image and likeness* we could have learned that we are words, and all that is required of us is that we incarnate them, fully.

If the word creates, perhaps it is our creative nature that was being emphasized—and what have we created?

Universe, from the Indo-European root *wer,* to turn, bend, from which Germanic *werth,* Old English *weard,* toward, inward, and *weorth,* worth, valuable . . . and the Latin *vertere,* to turn, *versare,* verse, version, universe.

The ancient Mesoamerican metaphor of "hearing the blood" is still alive in the shamanic practices, where "blood" is the location of the spirit, and thus it is "an animate substance, capable, in some individuals of sending signals or speaking." The shaman can hear either his own blood or that of others.

". . . the blood passes from the heart and 'talks' at the joints, revealing the conditions and needs of the 'heart,' the curer only need 'listen to what the blood wants.'"

Barbara Tedlock, Time and the Highland Maya

A wor(l)d that does not honor creation, that does not hear the working of words, nor distinguish between truth and lies?

Truth becomes a lie and lies truth.

But to see destruction brings another side to sight.

Being part of the truth, a lie can only increase it.

Hate is forked love say the Guaraní.

mentira   lies:
tira o rompe la mente   tear the mind apart

"You are aware that speech signifies all things and is always turning them round and round, and has two forms, true and false?"

"All things are in motion and progress and flux . . ."

Plato, Cratylus

Language loses and gains its worth from earlier times.

Christ said: *What comes out of the mouth poisons man, not what goes into it.*

For E. Fenollosa, the anemia of modern speech arises from the feeble cohesive force of our phonetic symbols that no longer obviously display the metaphors that gave them birth.

For Socrates, the most imperfect state of a language is one which does not use appropriate likenesses.

For Heidegger, we do not see in language because we do not see in being, and it is the destruction of the relation to being that has impoverished the relation to language.

But that negation can only increase our desire: the use and the abuse of words that have obscured their reasons for being will ultimately illuminate words themselves:

"Our ancestors built the accumulations of metaphor into structures of language and into systems of thought. Languages today are thin and cold because we think less and less into them . . . Only scholars and poets feel painfully back along the thread of our etymologies and piece together our diction, as best they may, from forgotten fragments. This anemia of modern speech is only too well encouraged by the feeble cohesive force of our phonetic symbols . . . It does not bear its metaphor on its face. We forget that personality once meant, not the soul, but the soul's mask."

Ernest Fenollosa, *The Chinese Written Character as a Medium for Poetry*

"I believe that if we could always, or almost always, use likenesses which are perfectly appropriate, this would be the most perfect state of language; as the opposite is the most imperfect."

Plato, *Cratylus*

". . .language in general is worn out and used up—an indispensable but masterless means of communication that may be used as one pleases, as indifferent as a means of public transport, . . . which every-one rides in . . . without hindrance and above all *without danger*."

Martin Heidegger, *Introduction to Metaphysics*

For Heidegger it has been the will of man to assert himself as the abso-lute rule in industrial and technological production and to turn the Earth and everything in it into raw material at his disposal:
"Man becomes human material, which is disposed of with a view to proposed goals." . . . "Modern Science and the total state, as neces-sary consequences of the nature of technology, are also its atten-dants. . . . Not only are living things technically objectivated in stock-breeding and exploitation; the attack of atomic physics on the phe-nomena of living matter as such is in full swing." . . . "What has long been threatening man with death,. . . is the unconditional character of mere willing in the sense of purposeful self assertion in everything."
. . . "the view that technological production puts the world in order, while in fact this ordering is precisely what levels every *ordo*, every rank, down to the uniformity of production, and thus from the outset destroys the realm from which any rank and recognition could arise."

"The self-assertion of technological objectivation is the constant nega-tion of death. By this negation death itself becomes something nega-tive."

Martin Heidegger, *What Are Poets For*

". . .our task is to impress this preliminary, transient earth upon our-selves with so much suffering and so passionately that its nature rises up again 'invisibly' within us. *We are the bees of the invisible.*"

Rainer Maria Rilke, *Letter, November 13, 1925*

When we speak, life speaks
Kaushitaki Upanishad

Wisdom is language
María Sabina

Sooner or later we will reach the consciousness of word-working, the shared knowledge that until now injustice and exploitation have impeded.

asumir colectivamente   to assume collectively
elegir juntos   el ser   to choose together   being

"But it is only in the modern societies of the West that nonreligious man has developed fully." . . . "Man *makes himself,* and he only makes himself completely in proportion as he desacalizes himself and the world. The sacred is the first obstacle to freedom.

Mircea Eliade, *The Sacred and the Profane*

If we turn to ourselves, to our own words, we will see that words always contained in themselves the ambiguity of being at once sacred and profane.
To *see* them in their totality, to know them (to be with them) would let us assume our own ambiguity, our potential to destroy and create.

". . .in the last analysis, modern nonreligious man assumes a tragic existence and ( ) his existential choice is not without its greatness. But this nonreligious man descends from *homo religiosus* and, whether he likes it or not, he is also the work of religious man." . . . "This means that the existential crisis is, finally *"religious,"* since on the archaic levels of culture *being* and the *sacred* are one."

Mircea Eliade, *The Sacred and the Profane*

"Being's poem, just begun, is man."

Martin Heidegger, *Poetry, Language, Thought*

In *consciousness,* we unite two roots, *kom,* with, and *scire,* to know.

Kom, beside, near, by, with. Germanic *ga,* Old English *ge,* together. Latin *cum, co,* with. Suffixed form *kom-tra,* in Latin *contra,* against, suffixed form *kom-yo,* in Greek *koinos,* common, shared.

Sek, to cut, split, Latin *scire,* to know, "to separate one thing from another." Old English *scim,* shin, shinbone "piece cut off." Suffixed form *skiy-ena,* Old Irish *scian,* knife, Germanic *skitan,* to separate, defecate. Suffixed form, *sk(h)id-yo* in Greek *skhizein,* split.

demo (the root for democracy), the people, comes from the root *da, dai,* to divide. Suffixed form *da-mo,* division of society, *demos,* people, land. (Those who divide among themselves what there is.)

"What is important is learning to live in the speaking of language."

"Language speaks . . . Accordingly what we seek lies in the poetry of the spoken word."

Martin Heidegger, *Poetry, Language, Thought*

Universe says: verse becomes one only in the union of every one, and of everyone and God.

Light, love, and language are formed simultaneously in the creation myth.

The word says: only by being one does the way *to those who redeem speech* open for us, giving back to the word the power to speak to us.

Every form has a force.

The force that finds its own vibration.

The word is the breath of love armed to inspire love for the great poem: creation.

"All truth has to be expressed in sentences because all truth is the transference of power."

Fenollosa, Ibid.

"'Is' comes from the Aryan root *as* to breathe."

Fenollosa, Ibid.

"The breath of life is one."

Kaushitaki Upanishad

Jim Melchert

GIVEN THE CHANCE to write about anything I wanted to, I suppose I would use it to describe what I did years ago when I realized that I had to rethink the way I was teaching. In retrospect it seems that I revised my approach systematically and efficiently, but in fact it took me several years of following hunches and watching carefully.

It's not that I had been teaching badly. I didn't like what I was passing on to students by way of attitudes and values. I was shortchanging them when I realized they deserved better.

The incidents that help bring about a radical change are often small themselves. One such moment remains fresh. I was in downtown Berkeley about to leave for Kansas City where I was to address a convention. A young man came up to me whom I had seen a few times in my office. He wasn't enrolled at the University. Would I give him a quarter if he sang me a song? I said

41

OK. It was a slow blues sung sweetly and so softly that only I could hear. I felt as though I were being visited by an angel.

The University of California seemed over-sized in the late sixties, early seventies. The beginning courses in the Art Department attracted more undergraduates than there was room for. There would be as many as five sections of a course and even then not everyone could get in. As an instructor you would often have as many as thirty students in a class. If you wanted to improve the situation, you had to find a way of teaching that welcomed numbers, a philosophy and a format that fared better when the room was full.

Fortunately I really wanted to do that and eventually I succeeded.

It helped to conceive of *14A-Introduction to Sculpture* as an introduction to visual metaphor and to visual thinking. We would take one question a session to solve, such as, how would you make something heavy look light? How would you make something near look far away? You had to think visually to solve problems of this sort. Then I would divide the class into teams of four or five so that everyone had the benefit of discussing the possibilities with several other people. The teams all had an hour and a half to produce a solution. The classroom was our home base, but the campus provided our workspace. Just as the make-up of the teams changed from day to day, the locations they chose also changed. It forced a person to take context into account. Where you worked contributed in some way to how you would solve the problem. There could be distant views, open sunlight, a sloping terrain, and many other conditions that could serve as a resource. We were lucky to have had Berkeley's climate. There were few days in the spring and fall when you couldn't work outdoors. There was also something invigorating about being outside in good weather.

The time that each team took for discussion allowed for a number of possibilities to surface. One idea will trigger another. This approach exposed everyone to more solutions than they would likely have thought of working alone. In the time that remained they would construct the piece that all of us would see. Each team had to find its own materials for most of the assignments. (There was no way of knowing in advance what materials the group would need.) The team had to manage with whatever the members could get their hands on. The advantage of this was that they learned to improvise. They had to use their imaginations and make whatever was available serve their purpose. Once you learn to improvise, you can make a lot of things happen with next to nothing.

When the hour and a half were up, we would all reconvene in the classroom and start across the campus to see each construction. Rarely were any two of them alike. Some solved the problem better than others and we would discuss why. We would see all of them before the end of the period and dismantle them before we left. (Learning to work as a team took some time. Authorship of the idea was sometimes disputed. The worst problem was the individual who insisted on having his or her own way or the bully who forced it. It took concentration to function as a team.)

The last half hour of viewing the projects was suspenseful. I liked the excitement of people who could hardly wait until you saw theirs, they were so proud of it. I still recall some particularly good pieces. Beginning students will frequently surprise you with their inventiveness. You wish they had enough experience to realize how well they performed. I've often seen better work from them than from graduate students. The reason is that they are relatively free of preconceptions. They have no idea of how something is supposed to look. They only focus on solving the problem. Preconceptions of what you're looking at can prevent you from perceiving it accurately. Artists deal with this problem all the time. A great deal of art has to do with shattering pre-conceptions.

Each term brought a chance to do things a little differently. Each class has its own chemistry and range of talent. I was lucky to be teaching at Berkeley where you could always count on the undergraduates being bright. Their parents had reason to be proud of them and often I wished I could congratulate them on how well they had brought up their children.

There were terms when I would include more individual assignments to be done as homework over the weekend. Often it gave a person a chance to redo one of the team problems in a way that hadn't been tried. When there was homework we

started the week by looking at all of it at once, having an exhibition in mind rather than a critique.

The assignments that I gave for independent work were aimed
at helping the students rediscover things they had enjoyed doing
as children, that exercised their aesthetic sensibility. I had to
draw on my own experience there. For example, I remember
that I used to pocket pretty little stones that caught my eye on
hikes into the country. I kept my collection in a cigar box and
got it out to look at from time to time, discarding some when I
added others. One assignment corresponded with this. It had to
do with making a miniature museum in a cigar box. It was to
house a collection of found objects that were beautiful and
engaging, but of no other value.

We were our own audience for what we presented. I wanted
students to address their work to the rest of us, not to direct
their efforts to an unknown someone somewhere. Being in touch
with your listeners affects what you do and what you won't do as
well. It helps you stay focused and can even improve the quality
of your work.

There was a point in those courses when we would discover
that we belonged to one another in the sense that we were inter-
dependent, if only for a few more weeks. The group had a center that wasn't an individual but more like a reason for being.
Students gave generously to it and worked to keep the momentum going. The class would even organize parties on weekends
so that we could extend our time together. You hear people talk

about "where it's at," "it" usually being somewhere else. During those last years of 14A classes, I experienced over and over again how we had made where we were the center of things, where "it" was happening. Artists know about this when work is going well in the privacy of their studios. I was glad to find that it was also possible within the context of a university classroom.

The lower division art courses had their counterparts in the upper division. In those days you could have graduate students enrolled in those classes as well as upper division students. Most of them had independent sculpture projects of their own in progress so that classwork was largely supplementary. Each instructor could choose how best to use that time when everyone came together from their separate work areas.

I used what I had learned in my lower division section and devoted the time to doing in groups what we couldn't do alone. All of our activity was directed at exercising the imagination. It was like a calisthenics class in which you had to stretch. I needed that sort of workout as much as anyone else. We essentially played and went about it as seriously as children do. Playing is a strategy for investigating situations and options that you don't yet understand. To refer to my childhood again, I remember how intensely I played magician for weeks after my parents had taken me to see a performance by Blackstone, an amazing stage magician. Children will investigate being the school nurse or being a cricket by acting out the part in their play.

The so-called advanced students were getting plenty of instruction in the materials and techniques of sculpturemaking in their other courses. What I wanted to give them were the means for keeping in touch with themselves. I wanted them to respect their experience and draw on it as a resource. They got permission from me to do this, which leads to the next and more important step, i.e. giving themselves the permission to re-establish identity with the child in them whose powers of imagination could work miracles.

As for the issues we involved ourselves with, we worked at many over the years, such as the conventions of doing something. By that I mean what remain as constants in any activity and what the variables are. We recognize product by its conventions. I liked to examine any question in the most familiar territory. Storytelling lent itself well to understanding conventions and how to play with them, so we frequently started there.

Now isn't the time to go into the richness of people's stories. It's enough to note that a group can do a great deal with a simple beginning. You can improvise freely with content, formal structures, sound, and as many aspects as your imagination detects. Imagination is an astounding gift. It's like having an additional pair of eyes that see connections and opportunities where there would appear to be none. I'm very concerned about keeping the imagination active. The less you use it, the more you let other people determine your values.

A great asset at the time was a nearby room that we cleared and called "The White Room." It stayed empty, a square space with lighting and four bare walls. It could become anything we needed it for, the sort of versatile, containing space that you want when you're improvising. We worked on pieces there that dealt with time, rhythm, repetition, and other considerations of aesthetic merit.

Much of what we did must have bordered on the ludicrous, but you have to learn to let yourself take such risks. My students trusted me and took the assignments as seriously as I handed them out. No one ever said to me, "You've got to be kidding," although it must have crossed many a mind in the early weeks of a course.

The most encouraging reinforcement that I got from another artist in those days was from Bill Allen who taught painting in the neighboring building. He took great pleasure in that part of your personality that remains unsophisticated. It's a part that we usually keep to ourselves, for good reason, I'm sure. Bill Allen believed that often where we lack sophistication is where we find a stronger bond with other people. He had found enjoyable ways of exploring this in his classes, two of which I relied on at various times. One he called Family Pictures. He had everyone in the class send home for family slides and home movies which each person took a turn at showing on the appointed day. We were introduced to aunts and uncles, shots of themselves as children, everything that you might expect to be tedious and even a little embarrassing. Actually everyone loved the session. It was as exciting as opening presents at Christmas.

The other event that Bill Allen left with me was having the class give five minute demonstrations of something each person could do well. Until I sat through one of these, I had no idea that so many people had mastered some unusual feat, often of no practical value, such as writing sentences backward rapidly. There are individuals whose ability at jazz guitar will surprise you, but obsessive kinds of accomplishments seem more common. I remember a workshop that I did in Missoula in which a boy made a lasso with a string and caught a fly with it which he then held on a leash. It's astounding when someone shares that kind of unpublicized skill with you, a circus act that he probably never thought of showing anyone.

The experiences I've been describing were quite wonderful years for me though I never expected to write about them. I suppose that makes me a little like the boy who could lasso a fly.

Amy Gerstler

Seventeen Haiku

"Eventually, you must choose one of them,
disappointing the others"

Five suicidal
librarians run their hands
through your hair, and sigh.

"Deposition"

Silent Quakers wait
in church for the voice of God
to fill one of them.

"Is this a caress
or a chokehold?" he recalls
hearing her whimper.

"With Her Last Remaining Strength"

The dying girl bathes
carefully. She wants to be
found perfumed and clean.

To miss the results
of my autopsy. . . how sad
I'm so curious.

"Things to throw at a bride instead of rice. . ."

Tiddlywinks, glitter,
sheep's teeth, raisins, dimes, sox, salt,
buttons, vitamins.

Faith has no price. You
see me standing before you,
refusing to leave.

"All That's on Hand at the Moment"

Mourning doves' spiral
cries and slight fever are not
much to offer you.

Little women will
easily mislead obese
bald politicians.

"Get Well or Else"

The false home, the sick-
bed . . . its tender mattress flesh.
Rise up! Come with me.

"Her Universal Allure"

I, too, would like to
kiss such a calm, pretty face,
then watch it turn wild.

"Departing"

As one goes, rain falls.
Still, I will honor you for
the rest of my life.

"Transition"

I want you with me
in the flesh as you are at
all times in spirit.

"Astro-Boy"

You have no feet, just
tailpipes, but that only makes
me love you much more.

The tombs of lady
doctors and physicists give
off amazing rays.

"The Midwest"

What thrives in this soil?
Artistic impulse, wild rice,
sinkholes and Christians.

"Water/Loss"

Gone gone gone. The thing
I crave skitters away from
the touch of my hand.

Housebound

When we fuck, stars don't peer down: they can't.
We fornicate indoors, under roofs, under wraps;
far from nature's prying eyes—from the trees'
slight green choreography, wrung from rigid trunks,
that leaves us unmoved. In full view of the shower
head and bookcases, we lick and tickle each other.
Every stick of furniture's a witness. We'd like
to believe our love's a private sentiment, yet
how many couches, cots and benches have soaked up
some? Lust adheres to objects, becomes a prejudice
instilled in utensils by human use. How can I blind
these peeping Toms—silence the libidinous whining
of sipped-from paper cups and used toothbrushes?
I can't. I wait for the outspoken adolescent spoons
to rust and hold their tongues so we can be alone.

The Unforeseen

In bible times heavenly messengers, disguised as beggars, were
everywhere. Divine communiques arrive nowadays via strange
mediums: meanings profuse and profound are inscribed in everyday
life's most minor designs: the way glasses and plates rearranged
themselves when our backs were turned, how my sisters and I
seemed to read each others' minds, and times when something in
the attic groaned at such appropriate moments: these were glim-
mers, little inklings, of what we longed for. At times, from our
window, we'd watch homeless men sculk around our yard, exhibit-
ing big discrepancies between their teeth. Father would send them
away. But those poor, prevented messengers! How could Father have
known the effects his protections would have on four daughters,
stuck in this small town few people ever leave? High hopes erode
here like houseboats sunk into mud at the bottom of an ancient
Chinese waterway. We offer God strict, intimate prayers, but perhaps it would be better to simply admit our helplessness and send
up waves of that agony instead. The homeless men paced under our
windows at dusk, sometimes singing a little: ". . .river Jordan is
deep and wide / milk and honey on the other side. . ." those lyrics,
in earthy baritones, sung by shirtless, sweating men, seemed to
beckon us toward unchristian vistas. Something in the thirsty way
they mouthed the word "milk" made me want to jump down from
our window, into their midst, though it was some distance. These
were sooty, threatening men, wearing huge weathered boots—whom
Father had turned away from our door. Men with cabbage or worse
on their breaths. Men on whom all clothing looked baggy and un-
natural. Men who washed by sloshing trough-water on their chests
and upper arms. We girls pined to be pinned down by something
heavy and gruff. One of us would sometimes rub her cheek against a

tree trunk, scraping her skin on its bark. There was one man in particular, less well-built than the others. At noon I caught sight of him bending down, across a meadow. When he lifted his head, sunlight shone through his ears, giving them a red glow, and I remembered the blood in him. I could almost see his delicate, hairlike capillaries, and I thought about my downfall.

The Soul Looks Down on the Body

Dung heap. Poor cooled shell.
Orange peel. Husk, crust, bark.
Armor my meat rode beneath. . .
stink-mobile with me asleep
at the wheel. Fleas' breeding
ground. Rigamorole of gristle
and digits. Pain parlor. Gate
left ajar. Walls of my old home;
I gaze back on you with disbelief:
How could you have kept me prisoner
for so long?

A Father at His Son's Baptism

Cutlet carved from our larger carcasses:
thus were you made—from spit and a hug.
The scratchy stuff you're lying on is wool.
You recognize the pressure of your mother's hand.
That white moon with a bluish cast is a priest's face,
frowning over a water bowl. Whatever befalls you now,
you've been blessed, in a most picturesque
and ineffective ceremony, dating from
the Middle Ages. Outside, the church lawn
radiates a lethal green. A gas truck thunders
down the street. Why, at emotional moments,
do the placid trees and landscape
look overexposed, almost ready to bleach away,
and reveal the workings of "the Real" machine
underneath? You're so quiet. I'd hoped
you'd kick up a fuss, scream and turn purple
during the grandiose, significant minute.
But what do I know? Hell, do what you want to,
it's your christening.

A Fable

A soldier returned from the war to find his village in ruins. Entering what was left of his hut, he tripped over his wife's still warm body, unmarred except for a bullet hole just below her left shoulder blade. He started to cry, and without really knowing what he was doing he unbuckled his trousers and fucked her, twice, hard, once each entrance. Sobbing, he pulled up his pants, picked up his wife's body and gently layed it on a kitchen bench. Wiping his nose on his uniform sleeve and sniffling, he smelled a warm yeasty fragrance above the pervasive stink of charred wood and cotton. He went to the oven and opened it. One of his wife's last acts must have been to put bread in to bake. The two loaves were nicely browned. The man slumped into a chair he'd made himself, without bothering to shut the oven door. "She'll never taste that bread!" he wailed to no one, as out of the oven's mouth flew an ovenbird.

The ovenbird derives its name from its unusual nest. Fashioned from leaves and grass, the nest sits on the ground and resembles a Dutch oven. The bird perched on the sad man's head and began to speak. "Don't cry" the bird said. "I, too, know what it's like to lose my kin. Because I build my house on the ground, as you do, instead of in the safety of the trees, last week my mate and our fledglings were eaten by a weasel." "You poor creature" the man whispered, so dazed and weak he could barely keep his eyes open. He felt dead drunk. Everywhere he looked he saw little black and yellow explosions. "My wife and I hadn't even had a child yet. We thought, after the war. . ." his voice trailed off and his head clunked down on the table. Immediately he began to snore. "Well," chirped the bird, right in the man's ear, "I can help you get your wife back." The man's head jerked up like a sleeping dog who's been kicked. "But," the bird continued, "you must do exactly as

I say. Take the two loaves of bread out of the oven, and sprinkle a little salt on them. They will turn into two pigeons. Wring the pigeon's necks, split them open, gut and roast them. They will become a pair of black, wriggling snakes. Cut each snake in half and throw the tails away. Put the heads in your wife's apron pocket, and they will turn into two ears of corn. Then your wife will wake up, healthy, except she won't be able to see, hear or speak yet. Roast the ears of corn and feed your wife every kernel. If you lose one, or if she spits one out, and you don't make her take it back into her mouth, chew it up and swallow it, she will never see, hear or speak again. You might as well have left her dead." The husband was eager and willing to do as the bird suggested, but needed to sleep. "Can I rest awhile first?" he asked. "Certainly not" the bird replied. "All these tasks must be completed tonight. If you go to sleep now, by the time you wake up your wife's body will have begun to decompose. . ." So the weary man did what he was told. Everything happened just as the bird had described it. At last the man sat with his wife like a large blind doll on his lap, feeding her roasted corn kernels. She spit a scorched one out and it rolled under the stove, but the bird hopped underneath and retrieved it. "Be careful," he cheeped. Finally the wife finished eating and opened her eyes to see her husband. "You're home safe at last, thank god!" she cried. The couple embraced and rejoiced. Then the man fell into bed and slept for eight days. When he awoke, he buried his bayonet in their orchard, and went back to his plow. He never hunted birds again, and when his wife baked bread, he got tears in his eyes but refused to explain why. As for the ovenbird, it flew out the window the moment the wife's eyes fluttered open . . . no richer or happier than he had been before. And he never spoke again.

Lifelong Dialogue

We inhabited an ecstatic landscape.
In winter quintessentially bare,
in spring visited by storms bright
and violent as operas. You promised
you wouldn't burn out first . . . not in words,
but with grunts, mutters, facial tics,
and cryptic postscripts. Yet a melody
came that spirited you away (you always
were a sucker for contagious tunes).
During the years I drank and drank
your advantage, I was rapt.
The outside world could jabber
and clang, wreak deep brown and purple
havoc, but I was right with you,
panting to keep up in fact. Arias,
monologue, yelps and dead letters:
perhaps they began to sound munched
and unintelligible. Yet you were
perpetually worth listening to, as you
struggled to fight free of false euphoria
and respiratory crisis. Sink or swim,
rain or shine, I wished, and sometimes
still dream, that in your sleep, by some
sweet means, you turn towards me.

See-Saw

In this picture, a well-read young mother ponders a paragraph in a magazine on her lap, while her child naps. An article on "The Riddle of Illness." Dry winds blow germs into the nursery by the millions. Window screens only sift them. They elude disinfectant and bloom in room-temperature air. A few float up her baby's nose while she reads, making the infant sneeze. Under the microscope, viruses look like corkscrew noodles, or other varieties of pasta, waving hairy little legs. *The earlier a syndrome is diagnosed, the quicker we as parents can face facts and make intelligent decisions. The waiver allows your physician to do whatever he deems necessary.* If she stuffs the baby's ears with sanitary cotton wads, it will miss Al Green, romantic maniac, yodeling and pleading, in sweet falsetto from the radio, *Call me.* The baby's eyes pop open. It seems to see the swarming pests, much tinier then the fly-swatter's mesh, that teem between floor and ceiling. Delighted, the baby laughs, its giggle a sound from another planet. It wiggles sticky fingers and rubs its curled feet together, elated, then sober the next second, as it figures out how each wriggle or blurt is chased by its reciprocal: a barren sadness. . . the wake left by every gesture.

Astronomy

It's hard to think straight with a cloudbound brain.
Desire, with its fires above and below my horizons,
burst into the room and caught me in the arms
of what I loved; but I held my ground—these acts
were no embarrassment to this ground-based astronomer.
When the moon's invisible, do those of us scampering
around down on earth resemble evangelists, or mincemeat?
Do the whitened bodies of women you've loved bleach
in a pit in the clearing, or are they catapulted aloft,
their smoldering bone fragments lodging in the night canopy,
forming a mosaic akin to a constellation?
After 4,000 years of mystic tradition,
the invention of water clocks, shadow clocks,
sun clocks and the engraved scale of hours,
human confusion still reaches dizzying heights
well before February (leap year provides little relief),
but at least the spheres hum their colorful mumbo-jumbo
quietly enough not to dismay their neighbors;
at least some of us are still sufficiently naive—
believing our homes the center of the universe;
and at least sound waves, channeled through the right
vocal folds, will still elicit tears, as in
"A sigh is still a sigh. . .", a line from
the song called *As Time Goes By*.

Fall

Outdoors, one season was leaving and another was gathering strength. It was autumn and many days resembled landscape paintings: wild, riled-up clouds, dramatic light. Trees still bloomed but were humbling themselves. Sometimes I felt I had a smirk pasted on my face, being somewhat unused to smiling and to having someone watch me smile. I tried to keep my expression in check.

We'd been friends since we were little. When I thought I might have a chance with him, just for a short time, before he went away, there were a few things I suddenly wanted him to let me do. Some were basic moves, pretty mundane . . . for instance, I wanted him to let me undress him. I wanted to see what his body looked like, and the way different days and moods changed its looks. I wanted to kneel on the floor in front of him and have him stand and rest his hands on the top of my head. Don't ask me why in the world I wanted that. I am not normally desirous of subservient positions. Some of these ideas came direct from dreams. I'd dream about him being in a certain room, with his back to me, about to turn around, and I wanted to be with him in that room, in real life, and I'd be willing to travel to find it, and see if the furniture in the room liked him as much as I did, and how it held his weight. Then my idea that he and I both needed to be human evaporated, and instead I'd wish to be a piece of furniture in that room he occupied, not worried about whether I looked silly or pleasing to him, just cupping his elbows with my armrests, as his flanks and back sank into me.

I wanted to lie with him in the just-cut grass by the filling station, that vacant lot, which buzzes and smells fertile and dry. Then the smell of him, of his clothes, of clover, bugs and daylight would seep up to our faces, and I wouldn't know in any given moment which scent to let take control of me. I'd try to see if I could really experience two sensations at once. I wanted him to sit down so I could sit on his lap facing him and wrap my legs around his hips. Then he'd be my folding chair. When kissing him, my thoughts seemed to be doing a lot of rapid zig-zagging. He'd find a place on my neck where it was excruciating—amazing: any pressure or touch, and I'd lose my breath, and immediately want to hunt for such a place on his neck, and also not want to move, just close my eyes and let him find other places. When I tried to read what he felt during those sessions, to see what he'd like next, or if he was having a good time, my touch became grasping, motherly, exacting; heavy with an odd attentiveness that disrupted things some . . . I wanted to touch him much more smoothly. There are only so many physical movements, and so many ways to receive them. Sometimes I didn't know what to do first, or I was afraid I'd die of terror in the lulls . . . so many risings and fallings when your concentration wavers or focuses and you want someone more or less . . . or you want them not to stop . . . or you want to be alone to think about them without the distraction of their swallowing and breath. So there were waves of warmth and excitement and strong comfort, and slow moments when I thought I might fall asleep, leaning on him, just for a couple of minutes. Then there were moments when I thought: I like this too much—I want it to be over. Much of this took place in public: in coffee shops, parks, even one time the library . . . because we were kids with no place of our own to go. So one minute I'd be swimming in a kiss, rubbing the backs of his legs though it wasn't cold . . . one minute overcome; and the next second, rocks of shyness would crop up I'd feel an embarrassed need to turn my head to see if anyone was watching us. Then another fifteen seconds would pass and there'd be a plateau, or a clearing, in which I'd think: Fuck being in public. Who cares. I wish he'd take his clothes off right now. Then more chagrin, and the sensation we were being stared at—as uncomfortable as when some creepy stranger begins reading over your shoulder in the bus. Then, I'd hit one level higher: the coffee shop would dim, and he'd fill the screen entirely, so I'd be unaware for a few minutes that the waitress had quietly set the bill in its little plastic tray on our table.

Pillow Talk

What's the best way to live
without flinching every minute,
or to lull yourself to sleep
when the laser disc symphony
isn't music to your ears
because tonight you want not
quicksilver but growls and
hisses? Think of vultures,
hippos, frilled lizards:
the noises they make, or silent
viruses doing aerobics under
microscopes. How does anything
begin? Did you originally kiss
me to quell the dread rising
in your head like carbonation?
"Tiny blades of grass point
skywards with forlorn authority,
toward He that sowed them."
I can't believe that either. Try to
be brave anyway. If the Titanic's
salvageable, then maybe today's
travails will leave a romantic
aftertaste, or provide a roller-
coaster of desirable side-effects,
like all the best modern medicines.

A Love Poem

Me Jerusalem, you Kansas City.
You fifth, me jigger.
Me fork, you canopener.
You sweetmeat, me bean-cake.
Me zilch, you nada.

Mark Thompson

Lining the Wild Bee

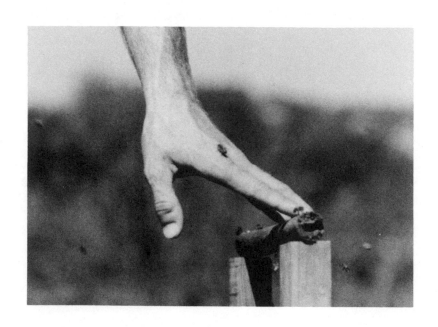

We had in this village more than twenty years ago an idiot boy, whom I well remember, who, from a child, showed a strong propensity to bees; they were his food, his amusement, his sole object. And as people of this caste have seldom more than one point of view, so this lad exerted all his faculties in this one pursuit. In the winter he dozed away his time . . . but in the summer he was all alert . . . Honeybees, bumblebees, and wasps were his prey wherever he found them; he had no apprehensions from their stings, but would seize them nudis manibus, and at once disarm them of their weapons, and suck their bodies for the sake of their honey-bags . . . He was . . . very injurious to men that kept bees; for he would slide into their bee gardens . . . rap with his fingers on the hives, and so take the bees as they came out . . . As he ran about he used to make a humming noise with his lips resembling the buzzing of bees . . . He died, as I understand, before he arrived at manhood.

July 1986

One of my projects involves carrying a portable beehive built into a backpack from San Francisco to New York City. My walking pace and direction will be related to the cycles of blooming plants and the foraging patterns of the honeybees. The bees are constantly flying out into the field to find nectar and pollen and they generally want to come back to the homesite, so you have to move very, very slowly—a good hour might be ten or eleven feet.

At that rate, it'll take a long time. . .

Yea. (laughs) My Dad was real quick to point that out! He came by and saw it a number of years ago—I had it all set up in my shop. And when the day was over, I found this note tacked on the hive. He had calculated how long it would take, and he came up with 121 years . . . leaving me with the question, "What do I think I'm doing?!" He certainly had a good point because, at ten or twelve feet an hour, that's just about how long it's going to take *if* I make a perfectly straight line . . . and I expect more of a zigzag movement. Now here's what I think's going to happen. Either I'm going to pass this on to future generations, or the bees and I will get better at this. That's what I think is going to happen—that each generation of bees born into this situation will know no other and will grow to respond more quickly to movement, so my walking pace will quicken to a more reasonable one . . . but, as with all the other projects, this one has some major logistical challenges. The pacing and all of that is certainly one of them. Along with survival along the way. And in a landscape that's mostly fenced in now, it's very difficult to have this sort of organic quality of movement across the country in the twentieth century.

July 1812

> For in the wilderness as was the spot, four men
> were there, and two of them had even some of the
> appliances of civilization about them. Three of its
> number were grave and silent observers of the
> fourth . . . [who] was extensively known throughout
> the northwestern territories by the *sobriquet* of Ben
> Buzz—extensively as to distances, if not to people.

It's funny how often someone who first meets me, or most beekeepers, calls them a Bee Man, and immediately you make this sort of hybridization of one life form to another, and forever more that's what you're called—it's less beekeeper than Bee Man. For some reason, Bee Man sticks. There's something about honeybees that people find so uniquely peculiar that anybody who messes with them, works with them, *loves* them . . . they, in turn, take on a set of attributes . . . I guess people who work with snakes are on a part, but . . . something about bees touches people in a way that . . . Maybe because of the general fear that people have of them, they think anyone silly enough or crazy enough to spend time with them, work with them, try to make a living by them, is already rather peculiar.

It's interesting, though, that among beekeepers—even the very devoted ones—there's no specific type. There's no Bee Man Quality.

There are all types. But I feel as though there's a quintessential beekeeper. For instance, Louis Dubay is in some ways representative of . . . a quality of presence, of charm, of gentleness that's required to deal with the hive over the long haul. You're constantly having to be responsive to another life form, sensitive to another life form. That kind of reinforcement year after year can have an unusual shaping power within an individual's life that will spill over into how they interact with other human beings and how they act in the world in general. And it's been my experience that the beekeepers I have met have been, as a general rule, remarkably decent human beings . . . But that hybridization of bee and man—Bee Man—there's something about that that sets a tone.

> *The keeping of bees is like the*
> *directing of sunshine.*

> Accident had brought these four persons, each and
> all strangers to one another, in communication in
> the glade . . . Although the rencontre had been ac-
> companied by the usual precautions of those who
> meet in the wilderness, it had been friendly so far
> . . . in some measure owing to the interest they all
> took in the occupation of the bee hunter.

What is it about bee hunting?

Well, it has to do with discovering an unseen source within the landscape. Getting one's bearings, sighting . . . and not just for food. A big part of it is just the process of searching. It engages so many layers of one's senses. It immerses someone in a set of dynamics of the natural world, ones that would not usually be required in a city situation. A sense of more fully immersing in the natural world. The early American hunters called it "lining" or "sunning" the bees—they'd stand in a clearing and try to catch the flight of bees into the forest . . . by holding one hand up to the sun and watching for the wings to glimmer on the sunlight, and the tracing the bees into the woods. The earliest image re- lated to beekeeping was discovered in a cave in Spain—from around six to ten thousand B.C. It showed hunters dangling pre- cariously off the side of a cliff on these very crude rope ladders, trying to get to a nest of bees tucked under the edge of the cliff. For humans to get at that—to gather the honey and the wax— they would risk their lives. Often they'd do it without any clo- thing on at all. There are still tribes who do it that way . . . They pluck their eyebrows to allow for a better sighting of the bees. There's almost a ritualistic preparation for this. Then, in parts of Africa, they get help from a honey guide—that's a bird who loves the brood that's left behind after a bee's nest has been taken apart. So there's a relationship between the hunter, the guide, and then capturing the nest. The tradition is that the bee hunter always leaves behind part of the hive for the honey guide so that the next time out the honey guide will continue its working relationship with the human.

A practical necessity? Or is it a mystical thing where "If I leave this for the honey guide. . ."

I think it's grown up more as a bit of folklore . . . so the bird and the human have this symbiotic relationship for getting honey so they can both benefit by this cooperation. Supposedly, if you don't share the spoils, the next time the honey guide will lead you to lions or snakes or something. But then, according to the lore, sometimes the honey guide will lead you to the lion's den anyway and then just fly away laughing. So the guide can be a deceiver too—for no apparent cause.

Who got to go out?

Certain intrepid hunters, or so I imagine. Certain individuals within the tribe who either had a natural resistence to the fear of being stung, or whose bodies had formed a natural immunity, as modern beekeepers do. Part of their protection was to remain chaste, at least from the time it was decided there would be a hunt until the hunt itself. Some places, they had to observe total silence from the time they got up on the day of the hunt. Mostly to avoid being stung. Because there's a kind of pandemonium— Psychologically, the act of being stung a number of times is a particular kind of violation to a human being. You can't defend against it. And tribal hunters, completely naked, were and are probably stung a lot. So I guess certain members of the tribe took to it and they were the ones who repeatedly did it.

I'm sticking mostly with ancient practice now—Given that bees were considered sacred by many cultures, do you suppose there was some kind of fear or trepidation about violating a sacred place?

Violating in the sense of getting the nest to take the honey?

I don't know the exact psychology, but there seem to be acts,

81

rituals, necessary to allow you to just go in, no matter how much you need it, and take something from a sacred location.

I know in India they would do a particular chant and dance, and sprinkle some honey for the spirits before they started cutting up the comb . . . but I also think it fulfills a certain psychological need for a human being to provide for his own kind. It's not so important what you're hunting as the process of hunting . . . of providing and generosity. As a measure of one's skill and prowess as a hunter, you come back and share the spoils with the people who did not go. Food sharing is such a basic bonding process with one's neighbors, with one's tribe, all those things. . .

> *July 8, 1977. Aboriginal Tribe Custom—*
> *tribe powders totem rock to dusk—thrown*
> *to the winds to change into bees for the*
> *next spring.*

> The three others . . . had come in on different trails
> and surprised [him] in the midst of one of the most
> exciting exhibitions of his art—an exhibition that
> awoke so much and so common an interest in the
> spectators, as at once to place its continuance for
> the moment above all other considerations. After
> brief salutations, and wary examinations of the spot
> and its tenants, each individual had, in succession,
> given his grave attention to what was going on, and
> all had united in begging Ben Buzz to pursue his
> occupation, without regard to his visitors. . . . The
> tools . . . of his trade were neither very numerous
> nor very complex. They were all contained in a
> small covered wooden pail like those that artisans
> and laborers are accustomed to carry for the pur-
> poses of conveying their food from place to place.
> There was a small covered cup of tin; a wooden
> box; a sort of plate, or platter, also made of wood;
> and a tumbler, of very inferior, greenish glass.

What I seem to do with my collection of books is to scan generations and centuries of beekeeping and try to pull out glimpses of what it must have been like to be a beekeeper in that age. The thing about bees is that they haven't changed much at all . . . Man has changed but bees are more constant. In spite of man's best efforts to domesticate the hive, to this day, the only bee is a wild bee. Meanwhile, the literature on honeybees—the quality of relationship that humans have formed to bees—literally goes back to the beginning, when the bees were seen as messengers from the gods. Honey was the only sweet, and wax generally translated into light. Cults formed around bees. One Indian writing says the eating of honey is like absorbing the essence of the Vedas. I mean just about every philosopher, from Aristotle and Virgil, down through ministers of the eighteenth and nineteenth centuries and even into contemporary times have looked to the hive as some sort of inspiration, some sort of reference, to integrate into their life view. So, in that sense, there's been a long history of looking to the hive for useful models, for metaphorical material applicable to human communities.

Of the beekeepers who wrote, and with whom you've felt kinship, who are the most remarkable?

Well, the most bizarre is Rudolf Steiner's *Nine Lectures on Bees*—he gave in the early twenties to a group of workmen who were constructing one of his buildings. I don't know how active a beekeeper he was, but he felt bees should be approached, to fully understand the hive, from a metaphysical perspective . . . that a hive was pervaded by love, that the binding force was one of love, and that until you began to see that as a binding force, you couldn't truly understand a hive or its relationship to the environment. He had the most radical thoughts on the hive I've ever read, and a number of them touched on thoughts that were growing in my mind, that had shaping impact on my projects. Among the more bizarre ones I recall is that the hive operates within the larger ecological environment in the same way that a brain operates within the human organism . . . that the head is somewhat like a hive located within a landscape. He said the hive brings to man hexagonal forces that are nurturing, that honey embodies these nurturing forces, that the hexagonal shape of the honeycomb itself transforms the honey that's stored in it—and also the bee. He saw this six-sided force coming from the natural world as fundamental to strength and health and vitality. I'm still trying to get ahold of that and really understand what he's talking about. He's the most bizarre of writers.

> *Bees have been able to bring what lives*
> *in the flowers into the hive; and when*
> *you begin really to think this out rightly,*
> *you will reach the whole mystery of the*
> *hive.*

> *So now, if one watches the swarm,*
> *still indeed visible to us, yet it is like the*
> *human soul when it must depart the*
> *body. It is a majestic picture, this de-*
> *parting swarm. Just as the human soul*
> *takes leave of the body . . . one can tru-*
> *ly see in the flying swarm an image of*
> *the departing human soul.*

An oak, of more size than usual, had stood a little remote from its fellows, or more within the open ground of the glade than the rest of the "orchard." Lightning had struck the tree that very summer, twisting off its trunk at a height about four feet from the ground . . . Of the stump, Ben had made a sort of table . . . and on it he placed the several implements of his craft . . . The wooden platter was first placed on this rude table. Then [he] opened his small box, and took out of it a piece of honey-comb . . . The little covered tin vessel was next . . . Some pure and beautifully clear honey was poured from its spout into the cells of the piece of comb, until each of them was about half-filled. The tumbler was . . . carefully wiped and examined by holding it up before the eyes of the bee hunter. All he asked was to be able to look through the glass to see what was going on in its interior.

The hive is like this extraordinary window into another world in a way . . . one of the most penetrating windows into the natural world. That I feel very strongly about.

You commented about Steiner, and the thing about love. . .

I should say that contemporary scientists would have a great deal of disdain about that. They would say a hive operates on a certain set of programs, really in an almost mechanistic way—robot-fashion—and when humans bring these almost metaphysical notions to bear on the hive, they feel like it's just entirely off the mark.

Why is it so often defined as love? What distinguishes it as love instead of just efficiency? What bumps it up?

It's so many levels. Every material that comes out of the hive is positive in the sense that it has a nurturing impact—the very act of honey-gathering, the cross-pollinization of flowers . . . it's a growth-oriented process. You have honey, pollen, wax, bee venom, all of value to human beings in some way, with very little waste left behind. It's a system economy I admire. It parallels my admiration for the Shaker community, the attitude with which they lived, the simplicity—every detail of their community having been considered and developed to, in some way, suggest the larger spiritual goals and aspirations of the community. The beehive is this elegant model of an organic life that feeds and touches everything it comes into contact with. I find it amazing that here is an organism that generates light (via wax), it generates food, its interaction with the landscape brings forth abundance . . . flowers, additional nurturing of the land. It seems to interact in such a an environmentally sane way, so sane that if the bees go, we go . . . Just simply interacting with such extraordinary material, that has so fundamentally to do with light, with life, with seemingly essential ingredients for life processes, even just the hard work, fresh air, and sunshine—all that is nurturing.

> Buzzing Ben . . . next turned his attention to the velvet-like covering of the grassy glade. Fire had run over the whole region late that spring, and the grass was now as fresh, and sweet, and short, as if the place were pasture . . . Various flowers had also appeared, and around them were buzzing thousands

of bees. These industrious little animals were hard
at work, loading themselves with sweets; little
foreseeing the robbery contemplated by the craft of
man.

At length, [he] found a bee to his mind . . .
cautiously placed his blurred and green-looking
tumbler over it and made it his prisoner. The moment the bee found itself encircled with the glass, it
took wing and attempted to rise. This carried it to
the upper part of its prison, when Ben carefully introduced the unoccupied hand beneath the glass,
and returned to the stump. Here he set the tumbler down on the platter in a way to bring the piece
of honey-comb within its circle . . . Buzzing Ben
examined his captive for a moment, to make sure
that all was right. Then he took off his cap and
placed it over the tumbler, platter, honey-comb,
and bee. He now waited half a minute, when
cautiously raising the cap again, it was seen that the
bee, the moment a darkness like that of its hive
came over it, had lighted on the comb and com-
menced filling itself with honey. As the bee was
now intently occupied in filling itself, Buzzing Ben
did not hesitate about removing the glass. He even
ventured to . . . make another captive, which he
placed over the comb. . .

"There they are, hard at work with the honey, he
said . . . "Little do they think, as they undermine
that comb, how near they are to the undermining of
their own hive! but so it is with us all! When we
think we are in the highest prosperity, we may be
nearest to a fall, and when we are poorest and
humblest, we may be about to be exalted. I often
think of these things, out here in the wilderness,
when I'm along, and my thoughts are *actyve*."

Within the hive, each individual is giving to the future. They
gather so much nectar in excess of their individual needs . . .
toward future generations . . . that they're . . . I think all energy
. . . all . . . you can't anthropomorphize but that sense of all
feeling, all energy given to the larger whole . . . each adding

87

along the way their own juice, enzymes—transforming the raw nectar into honey as it moves into a *common stomach* born out of food-sharing. Within this process, pheromones—chemicals . . . substances . . . messages, really—are mixed in . . . The queen, for instance, as she's being cared for by her attendant bees—they lick her, pulling off her pheromones, which move into the stomachs of the caring bees, then, through their food-sharing with other bees, this pheromone ripples out through the whole hive—helping to bind it as one. So food-sharing is really essential to holding the hive together as a complete organism . . . and individual bees are really more like cells of a larger form than truly separate individuals. Even though they appear distinct and independent, they are really more cell-like. This quality of exchange has a lot to do with the way I bottle honey each fall. The labels change with each year's activities . . . a reflection of my thoughts, my feelings . . . my own message of sorts. I try to add a little and send the honey on its way out of my kitchen into someone else's home . . . table—first full, then empty, maybe later holding some buttons or lentils or whatever—out into the community.

The bee first taken had, indeed, filled itself to satiety, and at first seemed to be too heavy to rise on the wing . . . however, up it went, circling around the spot, as if uncertain what course to take. The eye of Ben never left it, and when the insect darted off, as it soon did, in an air line, he saw it for fifty yards after the others had lost sight of it. Ben took the range, and was silent fully a minute while he did so.

"I must 'angle' for them, chaps, and if you will go with me, strangers, you shall soon see the nicest part of the business of bee-hunting. Many a man who can 'line' a bee can do nothing at an angle."

As this was only gibberish to the listeners, no answer was made, but all prepared to follow. . .

That sense of submerging one's ego to more fully appreciate and engage and be sensitive to the hive—that you have to sort of take on a different role of receivership . . . to get beyond the surface of things. Inherent in this process is a set of hurdles, tests, rigorous requirements that if you pass through them, other things open up or are made available to you for having sustained your commitment to it. It's fairly elegant in its simplicity—just the very act of sustained caretakership is so clear a . . . so clear a . . I don't know . . . a linkage to what I think are more fundamental forces of nature that our day-to-day lives don't allow much contact with. It depends on who's doing the looking, but if you can engage the hive, maybe with less preconceptions, it will, by its very nature, guide you through to something else. And maybe you can step beyond your own generation. My sense is that Man lives increasingly within his (our) own reflection. A lot of what my work deals with—over extended time periods—is really finding ways of throwing off preconceptions. My work, initially to build a relationship with honeybees, grew into an exploration of different ways a human being could interact with Nature . . . what ways are available to minimize the distortion of perception? . . . That's why the Live-In Hive project. It would start with my head in an empty space . . . a swarm would move in, build combs in relation to my head, and in the course of twenty-one days like that, we would just work something out in terms of a joint living situation . . . spirit to spirit, a relationship of touch, a direct link between my processes and the processes of the hive. I would just sort of go into it. And something happens visually that I like a lot . . . that sort of electrified field of flight activity. I'm trying to get as much of that as possible on film. To show that in relationship to the human head . . . Of course, if I were to hurt the bees, it would be a whole other ballgame in terms of risk, so it's really important to design this to minimize anything of that type to occur . . . In tests, during extended periods of viewing flight activity around my head, boundaries between within-without begin to quiver and then dissolve—the source of the vision becomes less clear . . . And you're dealing with a constant state of buzz. The hive is always abuzz. And then you have the flight pattern of the bees going through these flying tunnels and so you're getting a variety of these hum-buzzing sounds. What happens is I just go out. This is so meditative . . . it just quiets you . . . it just . . .

Is it very loud?

No, it's just a gentle sound. It's mobile speakers around your
head. Some sources are constantly changing. And you have this
steady state in the corner. All those sources . . . One of the
things that has always intrigued me here is the quality of dreams
that will occur for the duration. I would think they'd be fairly
remarkable.

Ben was not long in selecting a tree, a half-decaying
elm, as the one likely to contain the hive; and . . .
he soon saw bees flying among its dying branches,
at a height of not less than seventy feet from the
ground. A little further search directed his attention
to a knot-hole, in and out of which . . . bees passing in streams. This decided the point; and putting
aside all his implements but the ax, Buzzing Ben
now set about the task of felling the tree.

Great was the confusion among the bees at this sudden downfall of their long-cherished home . . .
They filled the air in clouds, and all the invaders
deemed it prudent to withdraw to some distance for
a time . . . So sudden had the hive tumbled, that
its late occupants appeared to be astounded, and
they submitted to their fate as men yield to the
power of tempests and earthquakes.

"As long as I've been in the business, I've never
seen a colony in such a fever. Commonly, after the
bees find that their tree is down and their plan
broken into, they give it up and swarm; looking for
a new hive . . . but here are all the bees . . . buzzing above the hole as if they meant to hold out for a
siege . . . comin and goin like folks carrying water
to a fire!"

I've always felt, from my earliest moments around the hive, a connection, a resonance to a quality of space—whether the intimate space within the hollow of a tree or a looser, atmospheric, particle space honeybees generate when they're flying about in large numbers, particularly in a swarm—a viscous, dance-like weaving—a set of whirling particles that exist, have a life of their own, yet can only live in relation to one another. That fundamentally what we're looking at is how things are held together—that if we could feel the energy that binds a hive, we'd better understand the inner rhythms of a nucleus, of an electron field—the flow patterns of transformation—the essence of composition. The hive works—there's been for me a very useful visual, metaphorical linkage. To simply feel that interaction has added a lot to my appreciation of all that surrounds me.

> *The notion of a life, a living being, is inseparably connected in our minds with an individual growing and developing. This individual may be microscopic or it may be enormous, but it must be born, and it must pass its individual course of life always remaining a distinct being. In the biological sense of the term, however, life is neither a mass nor a particle of living substance but a process: a constant process of metabolism with surrounding nature, a process of assimilation and dissimulation.*

When the tree was cut in pieces and split, it was ascertained that years of sweets were contained within its capacious cavities.

He was a bee hunter quite as much through love of the wilderness, and love of adventure, as through love of gain. Profitable he had certainly found the employment, or he probably would not have pursued it; but there was many a man who,—nay, most men, even in his own humble class of life—would have deemed his liberal earnings too hardly

obtained, when gained at the expense of all inter-
course with their own kind. But Buzzing Ben loved
the solitude of his situation, its hazards, its
quietude, relieved by passing moments of high excitement; and, most of all, the self-reliance that was
indispensable equally to his success and his happi-
ness.

Woman, as yet, had never exercised her witchery
over him, and every day was his passion for dwell-
ing alone, and for enjoying the strange, but certainly alluring, pleasures of the woods, increasing and
gaining strength in his bosom.

"A'ter all," suddenly exclaimed (one of his com-
panions), "A'ter all . . your trade is an oncommon
one! A most extra'or'nary and oncommon callin'!"

> *May 22, 1979. Visiting Point Arena.*
> *Working out back. All at once, some-*
> *thing changed—a subtle feeling, a sound*
> *quality. Hive on the verge of swarming.*
> *A floodgate released: 25 to 35,000 hon-*
> *eybees, all trying to come out in the*
> *same moment. Like a flow of black lava,*
> *dissolving, then taking wing—forming*
> *these electrified fields of flight activity.*
> *Very, very intense sound; joy, release.*
> *They made a large, weaving cloud-like*
> *formation, 30-40 ft. across. Sound so*
> *powerful it filled the yard. I started*
> *screaming, calling the others to come*
> *look. A nebulous cloud, highly ener-*
> *gized, pulled together into a smaller 20*
> *foot mass about 6 feet off the ground &*
> *began to move slowly across the land-*
> *scape. I couldn't resist. I put my head*
> *into the center of the cloud & began*
> *running with it across the front yard—*
> *jumping fences staying with it. Now 10*
> *feet across, a clearly defined field, I was*
> *still running. Across the road, a large*

open field, another fence. Getting tired,
still running. Down the hill into a swam-
py bog-like area, my shins in mud &
water but still holding my own, barely.
They picked up speed & left me standing
there, in panting, joyful amazement. I
watched them as they continued at eye
level across the landscape. They dis-
appeared into the pine woods down by
Highway 1.

A swarm . . . it is a return to first
principles again by a very direct route.

"I believe this must be the last hive I line this summer . . . My luck has been good so far, but in
troublesome times one had better not be too far
from home."

I'm reminded of an experience when a filmmaker was traveling
from England and, through a series of odd coincidences, he
spent the night at my place and saw some of my projects under-
way . . . the Live-In Hive and some of the observation hives
were going . . . and his retelling of a Sufi tale that when the
earth is at war, in a state of disarray, all factions of the earth's
population at odds with one another, the Sufi's tell of calling
forth beekeepers from the four corners of the earth to re-
establish balance, to re-establish a quality of order, that lets the
whole live more effectively. I've never been able to substantiate
it with anyone else; nonetheless, as a thought, it engaged me.
Within that tradition, the beekeeper takes on a level of responsi-
bility normally reserved for more powerful positions—
politicians, the military. To call someone who was simply sensitive to interaction, to chemistry, to things working in collabora-
tion, without exploiting or undermining . . . just a healthy
balance of life forms. I thought it was an interesting thought.
And I live daily with the thought of how essential honeybees are
to our survival. The contribution of bees to the food chain lead-
ing into our lives is indispensable, and the survival of honeybees

is intimately intertwined with our own. Within my activity, I care for a minute portion of the link within that process, that relationship. . .

> The bee hunter left the place with profound regret.
> He loved his calling; he loved solitude to a morbid
> degree, perhaps; and he loved the gentle excite-
> ment that naturally attended his bee-lining, his dis-
> coveries, his gains.

July 1974

I bought my first two hives from Louie Dubay. One of the most wonderful, horrendous afternoons imaginable! You live around Louie and you see what happens to a person who's immersed their life in bees. Quite a fellow! I didn't know where to get bees so I called and he said, yea, come on over. He hides them throughout the city, in funny little bushes, on rooftops, in people's backyards. So we climbed up this roof on a ladder—it was late afternoon—he doesn't wear a veil or anything. So he opens the hive and he's pointing out the queen, pulling the frames out, giving me, this novice, the full introduction to the beauty of the hive. All the time he never looks up, and I'm running to the edges of the roof, I'm trying to escape, I'm being badly stung, my lips are beginning to swell up! He never looks up, never realizes I'm in a complete panic over there. He closes it down, I sort of scrape the stingers off and just try to make the best of it. He hoists the hive up onto his shoulder, we come down the ladder, and I'm in the beekeeping business. So, with two hives from Louie, that's how all this started.

He does get stung though?

He absolutely does. And his hands are so gnarled, it's probably like stinging a root. I don't think he feels it anymore either. If he was being stung a half-dozen times, he wouldn't let you know it. He just sort of goes about it methodically, indifferent to any sort of pain. That's exactly what you've got to become after a while. You just don't think about the stings.

*I first heard the fine, peculiarly
sharp hum of the honeybee before I
thought of them.*

Notes

Bee hunting tale: excerpts from Cooper, J. Fenimore, *Works of J. Fenimore Cooper: Oak Openings, Satanstoe, Mercedes of Castile,* New York: Peter Fenelon Collier, 1893.

Other Sources:

p. 76, Honey jar label, 1976
outtake from Immersion film project, Mark Thompson

p. 77, Letter by Gilbert White
David Grayson, *Under My Elm,* Garden City, N.Y.: Doubleday, Doran and Co., Inc., 1942.

p. 80, "The keeping of bees. . ."
Henry David Thoreau, source unknown

p. 82, Men gathering honey
Spanish Rock Painting in the Arana Cave, Bicorp, Valencia, from Hilda M. Ransome, *The Sacred Bee,* New York: Houghton Mifflin Co., 1937.

p. 83, "July 8, 1977, Aboriginal Tribe Custom. . ."
personal journal entry, heard from traveller

p. 85, "Bees have been able. . ."
Rudolf Steiner, *Nine Lectures on Bees,* Spring Valley, N.Y.: St. George Publications, 1964.

p. 85, "So now, if one watches the swarm. . ."
Ibid.

p. 88, "The notion of life. . ."
I. Khalifman, *Bees,* Moscow: Foreign Languages Publishing House, 1953.

p. 92, "May 22, 1979. Visiting Point Arena. . ."
journal entry

p. 93, "A swarm. . ."
John Burroughs, *Birds and Bees,* Boston: Houghton Mifflin Co., 1926.

p. 95, "I first heard the fine. . ."
Henry David Thoreau, *The Journal of Henry David Thoreau,* Volume V, April 16, 1853, Salt Lake City: Gibbs M. Smith, Inc. and Peregrine Smith Books, 1984.

Finally and most of all, for Victoria Trostle my sincere appreciation for your support and insight.

Susan Wolf

Recalling Telling Retelling

IN THE SAN FRANCISCO BAY AREA the 1970s were a period of intense activity in performance, video, and conceptual art. Terry Fox, Stephen Laub, Jim Melchert, Tom Marioni, Reese Williams, Jock Reynolds, Suzanne Helmuth, Jim Pomeroy, and Linda Montano are some of the artists who were working there at that time. In this context, a young Korean artist and writer named Theresa Hak Kyung Cha emerged, developing her own performance and video work and working in a variety of other forms: film, written works (poems, mail art), and slide shows. She combined a strong intellectual background with visionary qualities and her meditative performances and videotapes captivated viewers. Cha's work was supported by fellowships from the National Endowment for the Arts and the University of California at Berkeley and has been exhibited both in this country and abroad. After moving to New York in 1980 Cha found herself concentrating more on written works, culminating in her extraordinary book, *Dictee*. Her life ended in 1982 in an act of violence committed by a stranger, just as *Dictee* appeared.

Coming to the United States from Korea at the age of 12 in 1963, Cha had to acquire a new language and adapt to a new culture.

101

This experience gave her an acute sensitivity to communication, which is reflected in all of her work. As an artist she retained an Asian aesthetic sensibility that she combined with an extensive study of Western literature and cinema. Her intense fascination with language led her to read the modernist writers who work with words in self-conscious ways, including Samuel Beckett, James Joyce, Stephane Mallarmé, Nathalie Sarraute, and Monique Wittig. Beckett's work was particularly important to Cha from both stylistic and emotional perspectives. Both Roland Barthes and Marguerite Yourcenar (the latter in relation to *Dictee*) were, in different ways, sources of inspiration for her.

Cha's interest in visual communication led her to the study of film and film theory, involving semiology and psychoanalysis. But theory alone was not enough; she found it significant only when put to use in her art work. While making specific statements about the nature of media, her pieces always reflect wider concerns with language, time, memory, and communication. Her work does not become didactic or suffer from the constraints of a particular methodology or style because it always contains a deep unconscious and emotional element. While her work is an art of ideas, she did not reject the "retinal" aspect, as Marcel Duchamp proposed; her work retains an ineffable beauty, an Asian aesthetic, and a particularly sensitive feeling for black and white contrasts in images and on the printed page.

In the early '70s, while still a student at the University of California at Berkeley, Cha began to work as a performance artist with the encouragement of artist and teacher Jim Melchert. She gave several performances in the Bay Area, at the university, at the San Francisco Museum of Modern Art, and at alternative spaces including La Mamelle, Bluxome Street, and Fort Mason. As with much of the performance work of that era, all that remains of these performances are still photographs, some schematic scripts, slides, and the accounts of viewers. What we cannot recreate is the compelling atmosphere generated by the very precise choreography of these different elements. In her performances Cha combined film, video, still images on slides, her own voice (taped and live), objects, words made into objects, and movement. She did not try to express any one fixed meaning or truth but instead tried to capture the experiential quality of time, memory, and language. While her work was dense in its combination of media, it had a minimal quality due to the great control exercised over each element.

One of Cha's outstanding performances was *Reveillé dans la Brume;* it was held at the Fort Mason Art Center in San Francisco in 1979. This piece took place in a large, completely darkened loft. It involved lap-dissolve projections, synchronous interaction with them by Cha, live voices and pre-recorded voiceovers, and a controlled distribution of light. Cha stood in the center of the space at some distance from the audience. She lit a match and circled her arm until it went out. A tape then began with brief poetic words spoken by Cha about light and the feeling of light and darkness; another voice, the voice of Bernadette Cha speaking with Cha emerged from the darkness saying: "Now? Not now. Now? Not yet? Now? Not just yet. And now? Not quite yet. How about now? Not quite at this moment. What about now? Not right at this time. And now? Not this time." At this point the light began to be raised, and then was slowly raised and lowered while Cha's voice continued: "Absolute silence. Reduced silence. Guarded silence. Bound to silence. To pass over something in silence. To pass under something in silence."

Projectors were then turned on showing five-second dissolves of words on slides. They were projected onto a white door located in the center back wall. Slides of another door (ten-second dissolves) were then also projected. The first set of slides was in color—straight-on shots of a door gradually opening as the camera zoomed in. This ended with a long shot. At this point, the slides changed to negative images, and the movement was reversed from long shot to close-up shot as the door slowly closed. Cha then entered the image from the middle of the space, began to walk very slowly into the image, and became part of the projection in shadow. She moved synchronously with the door, moving farther and farther in, while a tape was played. The final track ended when Cha was close to the wall, to the large image of the closed door. Everything faded to black as Cha's recorded voice spoke:

> Be this word somewhere before this word   between this
> word   just before this word   even before this word
> even before word begins just   before this word ends some-
> where once   before this word said   this word written be-
> fore sound formed this gesture the last breath taken before
> uttered before reaching ears   when it leaves before the wind
> becomes felt   and ends there   and not end there at all

In this performance, Cha conveyed much of what she tried to examine in all of her work: the nature of movement itself and, in Cha's words, "a specific, isolated time and space between two images when a dissolve occurs, and the perceptual and psychological effects of those processes on viewers." She tried to explore the quality of moments "in between," of time passing, of words traveling from one person to another. It was the subtle relation of the words, the movement, and the light that were vitally important in conveying the complexity of the experience of time.

For Cha the "final" products (single images, single words) always remained limited, only shreds of evidence of more complex processes, shadows of what was really experienced. Much of the performance's power derived from Cha's narration, her extremely soft but emotionally resonant voice, and the elaborate control of the timing of the dissolves, the fading in and out of light in the room, and the manipulation and layering of images and shadow.

Reveillé was a beginning of a use of language that Cha elaborated more fully in later video and written works. Naming the "kinds" of silence touched upon the same theme: trying to locate some meaning in the in-between. One word is set out with different modifiers showing varied uses of that word in an attempt to grasp more subtle, shifting, multiple meanings. By showing the relationships between these meanings Cha sought to express a deeper sense of the nature of language and communication.

This quest to identify and somehow embody unnameable experiences and to transcend purely objective experience was a central issue for Cha. In her studies of film theory, she became interested in the ways in which film produces an impression of reality that manipulates spectators to enter into the cinematic experience as in a prehypnotic trance, in a psychologically regressed condition. While a graduate student in art at Berkeley, she expanded her work through study with Bertrand Augst of the French and Comparative Literature Departments and went on to study in Paris with film theoreticians Christian Metz, Raymond Bellour, and Thierry Kuntzel. As an extension of this research, she edited an anthology of writing entitled *Apparatus, Cinematographic Apparatus: Selected Writings* (Tanam Press, 1980). It contains several important articles, including those by Roland Barthes, Thierry Kuntzel, Christian Metz, Bertrand Augst, Marc Vernet, and Jean-Louis Baudry, as well as papers by filmmakers Dziga Vertov, Maya Deren, and Jean-

Marie Straub and Danièle Huillet. All of these theoreticians and filmmakers attack the traditional forms of cinema. A major focus of their work is the analysis and undermining of the traditional narrative, which creates a passively perceiving subject. Some film-makers have tried to disrupt this passive, dreamlike state by alter-ing the structure of the narrative and exposing the very apparatus of cinema itself, including the technical aspects of the camera, film, and projector.

Two major articles addressing these questions are found in Cha's collection: "Ideological Effects of the Basic Cinematographic Apparatus" and "The Apparatus," both by Jean-Louis Baudry. Baudry points out that the camera itself is based on Western Renaissance perspective, which locates the view at a fixed center, nullifying the possibility of multiple points of view. The movie camera would seem to transcend this limitation precisely because it provides, not one image as a still photograph does, but a series of images. However, the projector and screen restore continuity and arc used, along with other things, to create the impression of real-ity. The differences between the frames and potentially different points of view are effaced to sustain this continuity and the experi-ence of the viewer as a unified subject receiving a linear narrative.

In the videotapes *Exilee Temps Morts* (1981) and *Passages Paysages* (1979) Cha sought to break the hypnotic hold of the cinematic spectacle. Pictures of objects, places, and people are constantly interspersed with images of words. Words are treated as physical things in much of Cha's work. In her performances words are pro-jected on slides over images, printed on objects that were manip-ulated, and projected onto a film screen. In the videotapes words are broken up, the same words in different languages are juxta-posed, and multiple variations of words related by sound and meaning are produced, playing again on delicate movements and changes in meaning.

On the visual level, Cha focused on precisely those special effects that the traditional cinema seeks to hide in its attempt to produce a seamless impression of reality: lap-dissolves and fades. She extends her exploration of this form from her performances into video, where very slow lap-dissolves and fades are skillfully manipulated and totally exposed, in order to study their effect, to make them utterly visible, and to make the spectator aware of the transitions and of the passage of time. Words are transformed slowly into other words; as they change we catch them in that elusive in-between state, once again touching upon the usually invisible transitional states of process. Words overlap and change meanings, then re-emerge whole and singular again, only to disintegrate once more.

Fade-ins and outs are extended from the performances into the videotapes, breaking with traditional visual continuity. By fracturing and layering images of words, images of objects, and spoken words, Cha tried to establish new relationships between these forms of communication.

Another significant article included in *Apparatus* is "Le Defilement: A View in Closeup," by Thierry Kuntzel. It is linked by Bertrand Augst in his contribution to *Apparatus*, "The Defilement into the Look. . .," with some of the work of Raymond Bellour. The important feature here for Cha's work was the attempt in both Kuntzel's article and Bellour's "The Unattainable Text" (*Screen* 16, no. 3, Autumn 1975) to describe the nature of the movement of the film strip in producing a film projection. Bellour points out that the film is an unquotable text, the still images, the frames, cannot give us the full moments of film that are irretrievably in movement and operating on several levels at once, both visually and aurally. Kuntzel uses an animated film by Peter Foldes, *Appetit d'oiseau,* to illuminate the crucial nature of movement in film. The film-projection moves the still images, the frames, and at the same time effaces them and their differences. In Foldes's animated film this phenomena is shown in an exaggerated way: "Everything is constantly transformed in an uninterrupted graphic production; barely formed, each drawing is deformed into a new one and so on."[1] The images—as in all film—slip by at 24 frames per second, and the movement erases the process and conceals the images, which however always have a subliminal unconscious effect. It is exactly this process that Cha holds onto with her slow fade-ins and -outs and dissolves, trying to lay bare the techniques and to examine their perceptual and psychological effects on the spectator.

Cha was also greatly influenced by experimental filmmakers, including Alain Resnais and Marguerite Duras in addition to other more classical but highly original filmmakers like Carl Dreyer and Robert Bresson. All of them rejected a linear narrative and manipulated the experience of time in varying ways. In Dziga Vertov's statements published in *Apparatus,* "The Vertov Papers" and "Film

Directors. A Revolution," he expresses his aim to "break the laws of editing," if necessary juxtaposing images out of chronological order, shooting in many different ways from different angles, altering the speed of the image, and so on. For Vertov, "Kino-Eye is the overcoming of time, a visual bond between chronologically separated phenomena. Kino-Eye is concentration and decomposition of time. Kino-Eye is the opportunity to see the processes of life in any chronological order and at any speed."[2] In Vertov's work the film goes faster; in Cha's the image slows down.

At the center of *Apparatus* there is a visual piece by Cha entitled "Commentaire." It is a visual interpretation of the ideas expressed in the articles in the book, using typed and written words, film stills, photographs, and black and white pages. It is a visually eloquent distillation of these theoretical concepts.

Exilee Temps Morts, which also exists in a related written form in *Hotel* (Tanam Press, 1980), and *Passages Paysages* study the themes of the past and memory. Although separated from her native Korea as a child, Cha's sense of having a self formed in part by a past recalled only in fragments gave her broader ideas about the psychological aspects of remembrance. The Western concept of the unified self, criticized by Baudry in his study of the film apparatus, is also challenged by Cha's ideas of how memory shapes the self in complex, unconscious ways, continually affecting us in a disparate but profound fashion.

Exilee Temps Morts was shown with a film, of a room with a breeze flowing through it, gently moving bamboo, and a light curtain, superimposed on top of it. The image track of *Exilee Temps Morts* has a minimal quality: words are interspersed with shots of clouds, a white bowl, a piece of fabric, creating an atmospheric beauty that accompanies Cha's voice. A mood of longing is evoked for a past that can only be found in traces and fragments.

Passages Paysages (*paysage* is the French word for landscape) also conveys this search to remember. It is a dense, three-channel work with imagery of landscapes, rooms, Cha as a child, an unmade bed, Cha's hand opening and closing, stacks of letters tied up, a lit candle blown out, and words in French and English. There is a sense of struggling to retrieve the past, to gain some illumination about it, expressed metaphorically, both visually and verbally. The images are sometimes the same on the three monitors, sometimes different; at times the voices overlap but are not synchronous. The speed is altered on some, and the overall effect is an emotional intensification, building up to the expression of a plea, a yearning. The fades and dissolves give the effect of losing hold of the traces of memory. Cha gives us a visceral sense of groping for the past, not quite grasping it, as she speaks softly:

not gone
not yet
not gone not yet
a few remaining
a few
a few remaining moments moments
it should be as good
it should be as good as gone
good as gone, gone.
but still—but still remaining moments yet
still remaining moments yet
wait
wait what wait whom who waits where and when

In these tapes Cha tried to create a psychological atmosphere in which images and words would elicit unconscious associations for viewers. The symbolic quality of the images contributes to this effect, creating an aura of universality and timelessness.

Cha's last work, *Dictee* (Tanam Press, 1982), is a culmination of much of her previous work. It is uncategorizable, merging different styles of writing, visual forms, and kinds of information. On one level it is about time, memory, and language. On another it is about Korean history and it can also be read as an autobiography and biography of several women: Cha's mother, Joan of Arc, St. Theresa, the Korean revolutionary Yu Guan Soon, and Hyung Soon Huo, daughter of first-generation Korean exiles born in Manchuria. These stories are intricately interwoven as the text shifts from prose to prose poetry, from images to words, from history to fiction, and from past to present.

In 1979 Cha returned to Korea after many years of absence. At that time she found herself facing both her recollections of turmoil in Korea and new demonstrations. Connecting these events with her mother's experiences and those of Yu Guan Soon, she gives us in *Dictee* a straightforward account and also transforms these events by merging them with mythology, delving into further meanings through a lyrical exploration of the relationships between similar events located at different points in time. Suffering and misery are not denied, but the strength to fight and the ability to see Korean history in more universal terms provide a feeling of release and triumph.

The introduction of Joan of Arc and St. Theresa deepen this sense of universality. In searching for universal truth, St. Theresa was a model of transcendence of traditional roles and was commemorated for her egoless life. She found the spiritual in everyday life and did not waver in the face of adversity. Despite the tragedies and exiles faced by the women of *Dictee* there is a sense of survival, of ultimate liberation, of completion, as mother and daughter are healed and reunited in the end.

Dictee is also shaped by mythology. It is structured around the nine Greek muses: Clio (history), Calliope (epic poetry), Urania (astronomy), Melpomene (tragedy), Erato (love poetry), Elitere (lyric poetry), Thalia (comedy), Terpsichore (choral dance), and Polymnia (sacred poetry).

In her diaries Cha quotes Nabokov on Tolstoy:

> What obsessed Tolstoy, what obscured his genius, what now distresses the good reader, was that, somehow, the process of seeking the Truth seemed more important to him than the easy, vivid, brilliant discovery of the illusion of truth through the medium of his artistic genius. Old Russian Truth was never a comfortable companion; it had a violent temper and a heavy tread. It was not simply truth, not merely everyday *pravda* but immortal *istina*—not truth but the inner light of truth. When Tolstoy did happen to find it in himself, in the splendor of his creative imagination, then, almost unconsciously, he was on the right path.

It was *istina* that Cha searched to express in *Dictee*, eschewing a straightforward route to truth. Cha similarly found inspiration in the work of Yourcenar *(Memoirs of Hadrian, The Abyss)* for her blend of history and mythology and her striving for *istina*.

An outstanding characteristic of *Dictee* is the constant shifting of voices and the complicated self-referential use of language. This is consistent with Cha's earlier work and her study in semiology and interest in the filmic apparatus. Here she extended the examination to the literary and vocal apparatus. Throughout *Dictee* we are constantly made aware of the process of writing in explicit ways: pages of rough draft are included, a handwritten letter; punctuation is spelled out at times and exercises in French grammar are used to illustrate the imposition of a foreign culture and alien way of thinking and being. Calligraphy, photographs, and diagrams are also included. The physicality of speaking is made palpable in *Dictee* from the beginning:

> It murmurs inside. It murmurs. Inside is the pain of speech the pain to say. Larger still. Greater than is the pain not to say. To not say. Says nothing against the pain to speak. It festers inside. The wound, liquid, dust. Must break. Must void.
>
> From the back of her neck she releases her shoulders free. She swallows once more. (Once more. One more time would do.) In preparation. It augments. To such a pitch. Endless drone, refueling itself. Autonomous. Self-generating. Swallows with last efforts last wills against the pain that wishes it to speak.[3]

Cha's voice begins with this struggle to speak, to tell the history of Korea, of her mother, of Yu Guan Soon, and her own story through them and through myth. *Dictee* is a unique autobiography that escapes traditional forms and moves the subjective onto a universal plane.

In a short time Theresa Cha produced a great many works of art, only some of which I have discussed here. At the time of her death she was working on a film, another book, an aesthetically executed critique of advertising, and a piece using the representation of hands in Western painting. This diverse work is now left incomplete or is lost to us, but Cha's videotapes, writings, and visual printed works remain. In the face of the unacceptable tragedy and senselessness of her death, I quote Cha's own words from *Dictee:*

> Some will not age. Some not age. Time stops. Time will stop for some. For them especially. Eternal time. No age. Time fixes for some. Their image, the memory of them is not given to deterioration, unlike the captured image that extracts from the soul precisely by reproducing, multiplying itself. Their countenance evokes not the hallowed beauty, beauty from seasonal decay, evokes not the inevitable, not death, but the dy-ing.[4]

She says to herself if she were able to write she could continue to live. Says to herself if she would write without ceasing. To herself if by writing she could abolish real time. She would live. If she could display it before her and become its voyeur.[5]

Notes

1. Thierry Kuntzel, "Le Defilement: A View in Close Up," in *Apparatus, Cinematographic Apparatus: Selected Writings*, ed. Theresa Hak Kyung Cha (New York: Tanam Press, 1980), p. 235.

2. Dziga Vertov, "The Vertov Papers," in *Apparatus*, p. 12.

3. Theresa Hak Kyung Cha, *Dictee* (New York: Tanam Press, 1982), p. 3.

4. Ibid., p. 37.

5. Ibid., p. 141.

An earlier version of this essay appeared in *Afterimage* (Summer 1986).

Works by and about Theresa Cha

Videotapes

Secret Spill (1974), 5 mins., black and white
Mouth to Mouth (1975), 8 mins., black and white
Recalling Telling Re Telling (1978), 15 mins., black and white
Passages Paysages (1979), 26 mins., black and white
Exil E E Temps Mort (1981), 20 mins., black and white

Performances

Barren Cave Mute (1974), at the University of California at Berkeley
A Ble Wail (1975), at Worth Ryder Gallery, UC Berkeley
Aveugle Voix (1975), at 63 Bluxome Street, San Francisco
Vampyr (1976), at Centre des études americains du cinéma, Paris
Reveillé dans la Brume (1977), at La Mamelle Arts Center and Fort Mason
    Arts Center, San Francisco
Other Things Seen. Other Things Heard (1978), at Western Front Gallery,
    Vancouver, and the San Francisco Museum of Modern Art

Publications about Theresa Cha

Judith Barry, "Women, Representation, and Performance Art: Northern
    California," in *Performance Anthology: A Source Book for a Decade of Cali-
    fornia Performance Art,* ed. Carl E. Loeffler and Darlene Tong (San
    Francisco: Contemporary Arts Press, 1980).
Janis Crystal Lipzin, "Asian American Films," *Artweek* 13, no. 20 (May 22,
    1982): p. 8.
Donald Richie, "The Asian Bookshelf," *Japan Times,* July 23, 1983.
Moira Roth, "Toward a History of California Performance, Part One," *Arts
    Magazine* 52, no. 8 (February 1978): 94-103.
Michael Stephens, "Theresa Hak Kyung Cha," in *The Dramaturgy of Style:
    Voice in Short Fiction,* Cross Currents/Modern Critiques series (Carbon-
    dale: Southern Illinois University Press, 1986).

Peter D'Agostino

Parable

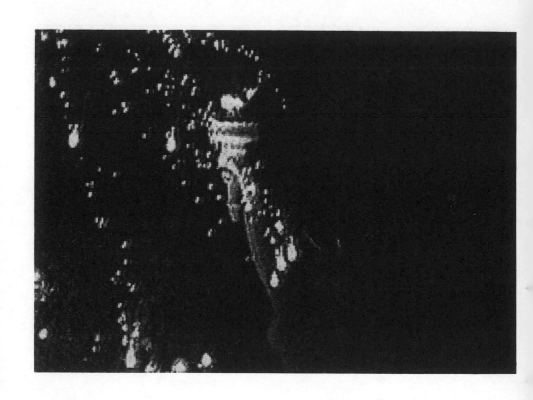

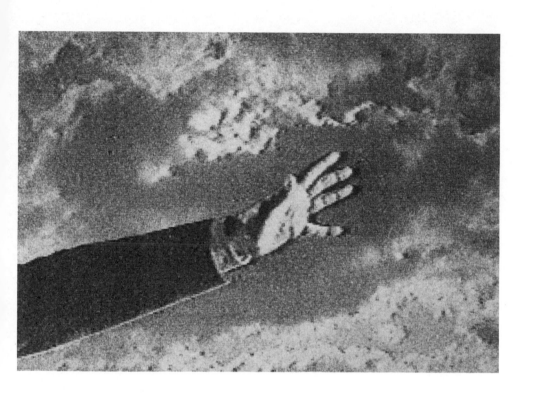

128

a splash. . .
this was
Icarus drowning

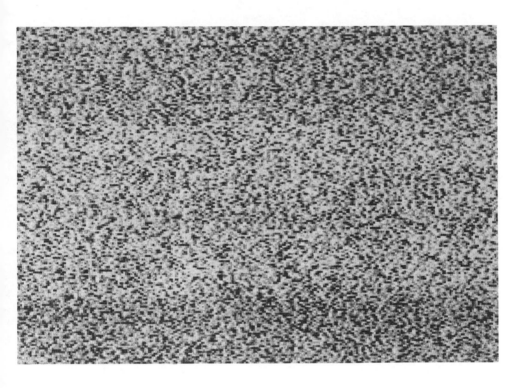

1. Pieter Breugel, *Tower of Babel*, 1563.
2. RKO Radio Pictures logo, 1941.
3. Statue of Liberty, 1986.
4. Apple TV commercial, 1985.
5. Breugel, *The Parable of the Blind*, 1568.
6. Apple, 1985.
7. Orson Welles, *The Lady from Shanghai*, 1948.
8. Breugel, The Fall of Icarus, 1555.
9. William Carlos Willams, *Pictures from Breugel*, 1962.
10. TV snow, 1986.

Douglas Kahn

A Resounding of Malcolm Goldstein

These petrified relations must be forced to dance by singing to them their own melody. —Karl Marx

If you cut an hermaphroditic schizophrene in half, which half would you take? —Dylan Thomas

What I have observed of the pond is no less true in ethics.
—Henry David Thoreau

The final piece at the end of an evening of solo violin was his own composition, *from Center of Rainbow, Sounding*. It lasted about twenty minutes, during which I had the distinct experience not of listening to music but of being present within a vivid evocation of nature. With a little afterthought it became clearer that it was an evocation of a *relationship* with nature.

It was downright bucolic. This was a persistent impression. Yet the piece was hardly an obedient pastorale. It seemed as though he was trying to ruthlessly saw through his violin with the bow but was unable to do so because the strings were in the way. Perhaps in this image, an idea of the repetition, purposefulness, cohesion, intensity and abrasive character involved may become apparent. Abrasion is, of course, what makes the violin work. Here it was as though the friction also seriously disrupted a surface of complacence. The intensity was seemingly an interpretive one. But he clearly wasn't interpreting a notated score. Instead it was a bodily

137

interaction with physicality itself. The instruments of this physicality? Reduce the bow to horse hair, violin to wood, strings to metal—an appropriate candor of elements takes place. The heat of this interaction, like a fevered Romantic interpretation, threw strands of his hair out into sweaty disarray. Unlike a Romantic, more bow than head hairs were displaced.

The sound at any one moment was of great density and complexity and, from one moment to the next, enthralling, expansive, oceanic. The image of sawing through the violin can be brought down upon the sound. While sawing a log the teeth do not encounter an homogeneous substance; the metal does not proceed with unperturbed precision. Instead, on a minute level the teeth are greeted by constant resistances from the cellular substance. The structure of a cell is violently disrupted: the outside is cracked, the multiform densities of the shell and interior are collapsed into each other. When the unit of sound is itself understood as a corpuscle the scenario sounds like this: the saw/bow meets each cell differently, and each cell is different, with results of great timbral and harmonic indeterminancy.

It brings musical meaning to a new pitch as well as a new meaning to pitch. The sawing, as an activity amid trees—violins being the children of distant forests—brought about another association, that of fiddling out in the sticks. The performance space in downtown Hartford all of a sudden took on the boots of an avant-garde Grange hall.

I should stress that this description, sawing and all, is for the detached purposes of description, and that during the actual performance the associative images were fleeting and much less embellished. Still, the images did occur. It was a situation in which the musician had to coordinate a complex set of actions while my own attention was undivided. He was busy sawing while I had the leisure and latitude to imagine it was sawing. If there were any coordinations on my part(s) it was between the primal brain stem and civilized frontal lobe, or at times the pulsed swaying of my head in approval. Although the performance setting did not invite a more kinaesthetic participation, this manner of participation was just fine, "For participation is a matter of attention and attunement and not of activity versus passivity."[1]

Also, as a spectator this perception—sawing, evocation of a relationship to nature and all—could have been the devil's work for hands with nothing to do but rub idle temples. Experience has taught me that my experience doesn't necessarily match up with what has transpired. This time it did match. The albums that could be purchased after the performance showed his solid attachment to the wooded environs of Vermont. Sawing actually was included in one of his earlier compositions. He's even done some fiddling.

On the first side of his most recent album, *Vision Soundings*,[2] is a version of the work he performed that evening in Hartford, *from Center of*

Rainbow, Sounding. The second side is *Vision Tree Fragment*, in which he rubs a maple tree limb with a stick and sings. *Vision Tree Fragment* is "Dedicated to the people of El Salvador in their struggle for freedom."

Having experienced an evocation of a relationship with nature confirmed but having no real idea how or why it should be that way, as well as agreeing whole-heartedly but only half-understanding the dedication of the rubbing of a maple limb to the people of El Salvador, it became personally important to discuss things with Malcolm Goldstein, then to give it some thought.

A few words about the words to follow. The artificially wide gulf maintained between culture and politics in this society does not foster common ways to speak about them in one breath. This difficulty is compounded in the case of Goldstein's music, or in any cultural form with a radical disposition toward nature, since such a disposition is historically the reserve of yet another way of speaking, that of spiritualism, mysticism, etc.—a largely phantom language which nevertheless concerns itself with very real human experience. So we have these three schismatic ways of speaking and doing: culture (the arts), politics and spiritualism. Discussing Goldstein's music necessitates an attempt to speak about or, rather, through all three.

To aid in this attempt I have taken recourse to a short, unifying piece of writing, discussed later on, by Walter Benjamin, the German thinker during the interwar period. I have also taken recourse throughout the essay of utilizing figures close at hand in everyday life: speech and dialogue. Hopefully, the reasons this was done will become evident through the doing. From the outset, however, it should be stated that one reason arises out of a compromise between the detachment of writing/reading and the palpable experience of music to which it is applied. Speech intercedes and overlaps here, having language in common with writing and sound in common with music. Another reason is that dialogue presents a familiar model of how things relate to one another—at its finest, an embodiment of dialectics. It also aids in keeping upfront the social character of all human activity, whether innard speech, international relations, or music.

One more comment before proceeding. Although some of my initial impressions may have been confirmed, this in itself grants me no authority. Thus, I may be more than willing to propound my understanding of Goldstein's music, but I am unwilling to extend my understanding to the experience of others. This should rightfully include Goldstein's experience as well. However, the very act of writing about his music makes such imposition unavoidable. You will notice in this essay, therefore, an oddly depopulated concept of his music, bereft of a performance situation and audience. In the place of performance you will find a concentration on the productive aspects of his music and instead of an audience you will find me. In other words, although the essay emphasizes, through the figures of speech and dialogue, the inescapable sociality of relationships to nature, physicality, and materiality, the way this is actually communicated among people is deemphasized. Goldstein himself understands his music differently:

> . . .as the natural sounding of the world (including people) and expressive within the context of improvisation (people being the valued center, in relationship—improvisation being thought of as the process/in the act of discovery—to other people, sharing).[3]

Please refer to Goldstein's own writings, in particular, to those discussing the politics of improvisation. Although he puts improvisation at the motivational and explanatory center of his music, I do not discuss it. The two works I discuss here are less improvisational, in the conventional sense, than his other music; a complete discussion would nevertheless require the context of improvisation as well. However, the cultural and theoretical unravelling necessary to do so is out of the scope of this essay. I do believe that what constitutes a "natural sounding of the world" is taken up here. And although the way it may be a communication *among* people is deemphasized, the writing of this essay may be considered as one way it has been concretely communicated.

* * * * * * *

Goldstein's music invokes relationships with nature, not nature itself. No leitmotiv of a force. Nor the stifling reverence of those composers who have endlessly notated birdsong. Instead, Goldstein belongs to the romantic naturalist tradition of Thoreau, who didn't feel compelled to bring the bird indoors.

> For sounds in winter nights, and often in winter days, I heard the forlorn but melodious notes of a hooting owl indefinitely far; such a sound as the frozen earth would yield if struck with a suitable plectrum, the very *lingua franca* of Walden Wood. . .[4]

Vision Tree Fragment, in using a large branch from a towering maple tree, speaks literally the *lingua franca* of Wood. This type of conversation carries to the turf of the violin itself, which carries maple and other woods within it.

Lingua franca, as all voices, have been molded in relations of domination. As peoples have colonized, so too nature. Now that the imperial extension has led to monumental social and ecological disasters, the assertion of non-dominative relations becomes exceedingly crucial. Seemingly, because nature's recuperative powers have been demonstrated to be formidable, it should be enough to demand a reconciliation with nature. Yet in present conditions this demand, no matter how distant itself from realization, is too weak. The extent of damage is too great, the momentum of destruction too ingrained, not to call for the resurrection of nature. The motive for this call can be understood as bald self-interest, if it must.

Just as speech precedes the colonizers in the form of mother tongues, there exists an immense chronological priority of nature over those fleshy cradles of human consciousness that now swagger the earth. A few heretics were able to sneak this realization into the inhospitable house of an-thropomorphine myth. One of the most endearing myths is the idea that a human-like divinity appeared only at the precise moment of human crea-tion, i.e. human consciousness. Having no image, this always-soon-to-be god could not create anything in its own image. The creative charm here is in its dialectical modeling of the eternal instant of—". . .No you first . . . No you first. . . No you first. . ." Prior to this endless deference, and during it, nature was in place. There was probably time for evolution too.

But the profane tale still holds. It is told within the opening tenets of philosophical materialism.[5] "In relation to the history of organic life on earth the paltry fifty millennia of *homo sapiens* constitute something like two seconds at the close of a 24-hour day. On this scale, the history of civilized mankind would fill one-fifth of the last second of the last hour."[6] And this, remember, is an organic timepiece; physicality is its calendar. So we're left with this trajectory before "civilized mankind" of the inorganic, organic, animal consciousness, and then a human consciousness and soci-ety which didn't subjugate nature.[7]

There have been questions lately as to the half-life of this trajectory. Before metronomes, the human pulse was used to mark time. But who's counting? Maybe a cricket clock would be more appropriate: the frequency of the chirping increases with heat. So with the glitzy flash of light, the superheated wind, this insect alarm sounds its sustained high pitched tone as human consciousness with all its trappings collapses uncontrollably back into its host. Or maybe the Grand Return will take the form of a puzzled, banal rot. It seems preferable to become practiced in a careful working back, not as a return but as effort to reinstate priority without destruction.

* * * * * * *

Originally a Brooklyn boy, Goldstein and his family moved to Queens and back to Brooklyn. He was urban landlocked again while studying musicology and composition at Columbia. When he was about ten years old he began to launch out on canoe and camping trips. In the mid-60s, during his association with Judson Dance Theater, he moved to Vermont with dancer Carol Marcy. Ever since, Vermont has played an important role in his natural education. It has been a continuing development in a natural milieu the way others, say, "jazz" musicians or fiddle players, develop in a social milieu.

> You have to really hear it alot, experience it alot. Live it. . . . You can learn how to play notes, but when you play the music, you're playing totally who you are in that living situation. So you have to really imbibe that culture.

He did not imbibe the culture(s) of Vermont. He tells a funny story about playing *"The Devil's Dream* or something like that" at a fiddle contest in Newbury and coming in last place. If there was a key social milieu, it was Judson Dance Theater.[8]

> Yvonne [Rainer] would do pieces where we'd run around the room. No one did pieces like that before. This was the first time people were doing things that we do everyday in our life. Walking, rolling and running. It drew me out to become aware of the physicality of who I am as a musician; the fact that I'm physically playing an instrument whereas before I had been playing notes that are outside of it. That would then lead out to a whole world around.

Judson's importance resided in breaking down the schism between his music and his daily experience of life as a whole, opening up the possibility of reconciling his music with his developing disposition toward nature. The imbibing emblematically changed from Yvonne Rainer's walking to Henry David Thoreau's "Walking," but the thirst carried over: "You must walk like a camel, which is said to be the only beast which ruminates when walking." (Thoreau)[9]

Internalizing the nature of Vermont was a slow process. An hour-long composition, *The Seasons: Vermont*, took more than ten years to put together. It proved to be a "very central piece to clarify what I was doing." First and foremost it was a clarification of what he had learned about *listening*. He could have composed *The Seasons: New York City* but "it would be a very different piece." A big city imposes itself. The ear, if it is to survive, must become muscular. The resultant composition might be as quiescent as *The Seasons: Vermont* is cacophonous. The relative quiescence of Vermont sets listening on its ear. "A whole different way of listening. In a place like Vermont, when you're just out in a space, you become much more attuned to the simplest, smallest or softest sounds. You become carefully attuned to nuances." The moment these nuances are revealed they command their own voice. At this point, then, listening unfolds into dialogue, a dialogue as supple and pervasive as what brought it into being.

* * * * * * *

The evocation of the relationship with nature occurs at the interchange of the materiality of the instrument and the biology of the body. This is a rough distinction; it serves for the time being to circumscribe an acognitive area, or—in terms of the chronological priority of nature—the precognitive where the musical material is generated.

* * * * * * *

Strange Strings was the title of the series in which Goldstein performed *from Center of Rainbow, Sounding*. As it turns out, the English meaning of "strange" trivializes the Dutch original. The series was originally slated for Amsterdam, organized by "a fellow in Amsterdam who directs an alternative performance space. In that context, in Dutch, *strange* means kind of a massage on the body. Implying through the word *strange:* working with a physicality." Physicality . . . there's the rub.

In *Vision Tree Fragment* he rubs a maple limb with a smaller branch. Over the time he's spent doing it, the limb has become smooth and shiny. The limb is about seven feet long, gnarled from knots and the bumps of age. It fell from a large tree—the Vision Tree—where he lives in Vermont. "The tree is about 100 years old or more, and about that tall. Lower limbs die and fall off. I stored this one in my wood shed for about ten years, because it was so beautiful, with no specific idea to use it." Because of the limb's unevenness, the act of stroking is musically somewhere between percussion and bowing. He points to a long length-wise crack and compares it to the split-log drums of Africa, the type that often talk. The crack gives the limb a chamber of air like the lung of a violin. It was opened by age in order that the limb could breath. There are also chambers buried out of sight as well as those which constitute the texture of the wood.

> The bumps are through age. Through changes like bodies change. As you turn it there are different pitches and textures that come out depending upon how thick the wood is and. . . . The whole thing constantly sounds and sounds differently.

The rubbing *sounds* the wood. Sounding plumbs the depths and back. Sound has the capacity to penetrate material, excite the unseen, resonate the surrounding environment, and then leave everything undisturbed. Sight must dismantle to bring the inside out: while showing me a certain area on the Vision Tree branch he figures it must consist of older, deader wood, "Because it looks like, if I wanted to, I could carve this out." The look leads to the touch which is more disruptive yet, unless it too listens through vibration.[10] The touch of the saw produces sound as the shell of the wood's corpuscles are warped and broken, as the cellular resonant chambers are obliterated. The sound is released to join the harmonics of the metal, then on to an acoustic space and other materials. When vibrations of sound replace the saw's teeth, the excitation still takes place but nothing is destroyed.

Sounding in its nautical sense is also a non-destructive plumbing of the depths. Long poles, lines or vibrations are sent downward to determine location. And the water is no worse for the wear. "Water is a wet flame." (Novalis) In terms of talk, soundings are the ritual insults practiced in Black America and the West Indies, if not elsewhere.[11] They locate, through verbal pyrotechnics, a person's location in community as speaker, object and/or poetic median. A guy nicknamed Boot tells his friend Money, "You got a head like a tornado mixed with a horse." Then there's your mother.

Your mother is (like) _____.
Your mother so _____ she _____.
Your mother eat _____.
Your mother raised you on _____.

Although there's serious impugning going on, it's a testing which falls short of actual disruption, a reading-in (and out) which never becomes an indelible writing-on.

Your mother tongue.
Your mother nature.

If a commune/dialogue with nature is to be entered into, speech must be attributed to it because it is not there already. This attribution of speech may establish the singular, corporeal presence necessary to come into a relation, but at the same time, by bringing nature into the purview and problematic of consciousness, it removes autonomy. Nature cannot fend off a barrage of connotation. This isn't an ingrained problem as far as relations between humans go because the attribution of speech—"speaking the other"—is constantly being reciprocated. Thus, when sound is sent into the cells of wood it constitutes a social impugning of sound to an entity mute to sociality. This act has (im)pugnatious potential, beginning no less a threat to dominate through its role as an inaugural imposition. Therefore, listening must become even more pronounced, such that the nuances assume even greater prominence, the stick bent the other way. The material must be given more voice.

. . .While I began to rub it and listen and to explore by turning the tree slowly, whatever, or different convolutions, then I began to sing. The way of singing was no way that I had ever sung before. Literally—I believe this—the tree taught me how to sing.

Since this in itself amplifies the attribution of speech, the inherent fragility of a truly equipoised relationship becomes apparent, as do the measures which must be taken.

> My inclination is not to take and see what I can do with it; I allow it to direct, by its own sounding, implications and directions to take. It's more a matter of yielding to the material than imposing upon the material.[12]

However, the dialogue, once set into proper motion, has the capacity to disperse any impugning of voice by the mediation of the voice through the material, by the way the voice "gathers up" physicality. Physicality can thereby permeate consciousness, opening up the possibility to progressively abdicate consciousness in a cycle toward acognition and materiality. Once established, this cycle can itself be sung its own melody. The resultant harmonics are those usually associated with a metaphysical contact with the world when in fact a more fundamentally physical contact with the world occurs.

Disclosing physicality through sounding, therefore, is a way of entering into this relation. If it was understood simply as a divulging of physicality per se, it would be just another compositional shot at birdsong, only this time from an interior, essentialist project—more insidious because of its unacknowledged human presence. A "being within the relation" is, on the other hand, an *essensualist* project. Instead of isolating a reified core it seeks immersion in a crux of flux.

* * * * * * *

Similar desires have occurred under the signs of "getting inside the word" or "getting inside a sound." Actually, these aren't approaching "the word" or "a sound" as much as an experience of "wordness" or "soundness." While a specific word might serve to anchor a sea of infinite meaning, the generalization away from specific meaning drifts in the direction of acognition. Meaning is not antithetical to "getting inside the word/sound." Any word can be saturated to the point of exploding through being infused with the history its traveled within, no matter how banal; this is how the experience can be socio-culturally informed, but the experience itself does not provide the information. The connection between a specific word and wordness also opens up a giddy plenitude out of singularity and a miasmic infinitude of interpenetration within a finite space—and other anarchic reassurances.

In 1916, during an especially momentous evening at the Cabaret Voltaire, Zurich Dadaist Hugo Ball recited his now famous set of sound poems. He prefaced his performance by stating his desire to get away from "a language devastated by journalism" and into "the innermost alchemy of the word." Apart from their onomatopoetic moments, his sound poems made no literal reference to an external world. They primarily referenced their own internal patterns of alliterative repetition. This manner of repetition having already been structured in—plus his desire to hoist the submerged secrets of "the word"—suggested a move, apparently against his will, into introducing repetition into the recitation of the poems as well. The repetition gradually became more pronounced:

> But how was I to end? Then I noticed that my voice had no choice but to take on the ancient cadence of priestly lamentation, that style of liturgical singing that wails in all the Catholic churches of East and West. . . . I do not know what gave me the idea of this music, but I began to chant my vowel sequences in a church style like a recitative. . .[13]

Ball generally maintained an antipathy toward the "primitivism" embraced by dada and the avant-garde at the early part of this century, often going to great lengths of denial to do so. For his performance of sound poems he could have easily sought, say, West African associations or ones from other cultures outside the West. Instead, he remained with the orders of chant, ecstasy and epiphany from Western religious and occult traditions.

Although the performance was but one evening, it was not a simple poetic exercise. Ball was not a simple poet. Around the same time as Zurich Dada he prepared texts on both Byzantine Christianity and Bakunin's anarchism. In his own way he sought a merging similar to Walter Benjamin's merging of Jewish mysticism and Marxist materialism. If Ball hadn't maintained an anti-Semitic streak, he might have sought Jewish associations for his sound poems. Possibly the 13th-century Spanish Kabbalist Abraham Abulafia, whose "science of the combination of letters," realized in ecstatic recitation, was an erotic science, like the alchemy that Ball would use to dredge the depths of words.

Walter Benjamin heard his own brand of sound poetry while on hashish. Sitting in a little Marseilles bar, immersed in a din of voices, language assumed the estranged character of a dialect.[14] This estrangement resulted from a heightened attention to the phonic particulars of speech. To this effect he was reminded of Karl Kraus' dictum that "The more closely you look at a word the more distantly it looks back." However, there's a couple of problems with Benjamin's assigning this dictum to his hashish experience.

The distancing it describes is an alienating one. Such alienation continues to be culturally invaluable as a means to pry social repression away from its naturalization. But revolution requires also processes of disaliena-

146

tion: disalienation toward the social bases of revolution, toward nature, toward commitment. Benjamin held the hashish experience to be a profane illumination by no means incompatible with political revolution. And what is illumination but a practice of disalienation? Kraus' dictum can be imagistically twisted to conform to disalienation, when the closer look and the greater distance resulting from the closer look are understood as elastic bounds to a world opening up to greater connectedness.

Another problem with Kraus' dictum is that it transfers the manner of Benjamin's experience from listening to looking, from sound (estranged speech) to the written word. The optics of such writing are largely inamicable to a more global connection with things. For example, although various activities may result in "visions" the methods themselves are overwhelmingly aural.[15] Or in sexual commune, the gaze localizes and genitalizes eros whereas listening disperses eros throughout bodies. Tocar. Ear drums are, afterall, the skin of a spatialized touch.

Yet the desire to disclose a word/sound cannot help but take some recourse to the fixity of sight,[16] and to the fixity of site. There must be a "holding still" so a common space may be occupied. This containment is accomplished through processes of spatialization, memory and repetition. The first simply brings about a sense of an object-in-environment through an apprehension of the physicality involved in acoustics. "All sound itself is a matter of moving the air; so that every environment also has its own physicality and the uniqueness of each space is what gives it that sound quality."[17] Memory attempts to drain transience, to capture a representation of sound.[18] And repetition "holds still" by employing the type of sequentiality attendant upon an optical apprehension of the world, draining transience by mimicking it with reiterated movement.

However, spatialization, memory and repetition, in their movement toward reduction, continually threaten to emaciate the word/sound. Spatialization through a reduction to structure and architectonics, memory through the fetishization of autonomous sound, and repetition through the type of redundancy found in capitalist rationalization and commodification. The latter is especially suspect, since in the current era of repetition repetition is easily complicit.[19] It can spiritualize systemic repression, counting sheep into a big sleep. Ironically, repetition has an advantage over memory in avoiding debilitating reduction, especially when memory itself is understood as a repetition. The advantage occurs by resonating a word/sound's autonomy against its mnemonic representation. Generally, however, this is hope against hope. For this advantage itself is transient, dissolving the moment it becomes anticipated. "When originality is lacking in repetition we have habit." (Søren Kierkegaard, "The Concept of Dread")

Of course, repetition is one of the more obvious features of the "minimal music" of the last fifteen years or so. Goldstein's *from Center of Rainbow*,

Sounding has been confused with minimal music.[20] However, in minimal music repetition takes its place in a general compositional strategy of reduction whereas in Goldstein's music repetition takes place as a means of proliferation.

> To me my music's not minimal at all. The word "corpuscular" makes alot of sense because to me every nuance of sound at every split second is very very alive. Everytime I draw the bow it's alive. This kind of pulse makes the whole violin resonate.

from Center of Rainbow, Sounding is a composition, or a "structure of improvisation," where repetition is not written by notation into the musical material, but is instead in relation to the material. And as with the impugning of voice, repetition must be initiated and maintained but also retracted and dispersed, lest it become impositional. Accordingly, the saw-like repetition of the bowing in *from Center of Rainbow, Sounding,* more brazenly repetitious than minimal music, retreats from being of any central importance. The process is similar to Godard's idea about stories in film: if you are telling a story very familiar to everyone then the storyline can be dispensed with and attention given over to more important things.[21] The decompositional process is attributable also to the compositional employment of gestual pulse and to the pulse set up by acoustic resonances. Finally, it is attributable to the way which the pulse itself is then diffused throughout the body.

The three types of gestual pulse in *from Center of Rainbow, Sounding* arise from the bow going up and down, from the index finger going up and down on a single string, and from crossing strings and performing multiple stops "making an arpeggiated kind of pulse."

> Sometimes it could be the same pulse from beginning to end. Sometimes at the end it becomes double time. So that's variable. Sometimes, again not by intention, there's this cross relationship which is for me fun, a very delightful sensation, where the finger is going at one pulse up and down and the bow is going at a different pulse. . . . and then after awhile for them to come into synchronization.

The pulsations, along with the repetition, invoke the repetitions of the organism: the pulse and pump of heartbeat, breathing, the strokes of lovemaking, peristalsis, labor, chewing, laughing, walking, dance, etc. And as these homologies are invoked they are diffused into one another. Coming into relation with such rhythms is often key in engendering various acognitive states. For most people, the most familiar is the intoxification of love and sex, a cognitive abdication which nevertheless amplifies a sense of presence. With respect to labor, Leo Tolstoy described Russian peasants in the field.

He heard nothing but the swish of scythes, and saw . . . the crescent-shaped curve of the cut grass, the grass and flower heads slowly and rhythmically falling before the blade of his scythe, and ahead of him the end of the row, where the rest would come. . .

The longer Levin mowed, the oftener he felt the moments of unconsciousness in which it seemed that the scythe was mowing by itself, a body full of life and consciousness of its own, and as though by magic, without thinking of it, the work turned out regular and precise by itself. These were the most blissful moments.[22]

Several years ago, Goldstein was listening to a recording of one of his improvisatory *Soundings*. In the improvisation he had arrived at the type of pulse that would later stretch across the entirety of *from Center of Rainbow, Sounding*. His wrist began moving as though he were playing the violin. "I was just sitting there and had absolutely no control. It was very frightening at first. The pulse totally became part of my body."[23] Coursing through the body, the pulse precedes consciousness.

In repetition breathing also plays a role: *breathing of the arm*—this is his term—but ". . .not linearly like breath in and breath out, but my total breathing." However, the breathing is supportive, not determinant.

Like ballet. When a person raises their arm they have kind of a cloud under here. Or they don't. It's either rigid, or it's dead, but if they have the right balance it's like a cloud. With the violin I'm not holding my arm up. It's just there. And this is a way of breathing. And that breathing comes through. So if my breathing gets tight, the sound also gets that way. If my breathing is floating, the sound gets that way, expansive.

Breathing, as a moving of air, flows into the moving of air which is sound. In this interaction a vitalization of physicality, and vice versa, occurs, acting similarly to the way the biological contours of the bow's repetitions reiterate, on an overarching scale, the physical contours of resonance. A harmonizing occurs between sound bodies: the lungs of the body and the body of the violin, "the box with the air inside it." The resonance of the violin thus becomes an infusion of breath, ventilated quickly, resulting in indeterminant harmonics (as weak as wheezing or strong as the rasp of an English washerwoman). This resonance then feeds back into the body.

If the sound becomes more something than something else, it might be not because I'm trying to do it but because there might be this one part of the body which all of a sudden just opens up. Or another part where this knot forms.

Sometimes there's a throbbing happening in the middle of my chest.

Nobody knows it but it's coming out in the sound. It's a high. An exhilaration. Large amounts of air going in there and not breathing any more than I would normally breath.

This feeling in his chest may harken back to an epiphany he had in the mid-60s while on a canoe trip to the finger lakes of New York State. On this trip he was fully equipped with Walt Whitman's *Leaves of Grass*—"language of the body, to be in 'touch' with." At a certain point he climbed Black Bear Mountain. "At the top, looking out over miles and miles in all directions, a fantastic sensation of my chest by my heart opening up and energy pouring out and out to the space in all directions. I am clear/so it is I am. After staying for a while, I descended again, drunk with the exhilaration of the experience/in-sight; singing." In a Taoist meditational technique of the absorption of breath, breaths are visualized as though coming "from the four points of the compass and the Centre—that is to say from the entire Universe—and one swallows them, forcing them to penetrate into the body."[24] Upon meditation each breath will yield its specific color, signaling an "integration with cosmic rhythms."

The head too, while lacking the elasticity of the lungs, is also a resonant body participating in the exhilaration. By opening up to colors.

Literally, at times, not all the time, I will see colors. I won't try to play the colors. I'll just enjoy them doing this with the pulsations. That's why it's called *from Center of Rainbow, Sounding,* the richness of the spectrum of sound textures and colors.

There is nothing mystical about this sensation. The colors are not a light which marks the flash of revelation. They are more akin to Yogic and Taoist techniques, where colors can mark the attainment of certain evolutionary states; in the more advanced techniques, specific successions of colors in themselves takes on significance. The rainbow itself, as a succession of colors, has less psycho-physiological standing than symbolic standing, especially in strains of shamanism where the rainbow is a bridge to the sky.

* * * * * * *

"To the Planetarium" is the title of a section in Walter Benjamin's *One Way Street* (1928).[25] Its two remarkable pages propose no less than the manner in which the *doctrine of antiquity*—"They alone shall possess the earth who live from the powers of the cosmos."—irrepressibly manifests itself in the modern world. Ancient people's "absorption in cosmic experience" decreased markedly upon the advent of the epoch of astronomy's "optical connection to the universe." Instead of an optical connection, those of antiquity practiced another manner of connecting: the ecstatic

150

trance.[26] Although Benjamin does not contrast optics with sonics we can assume sonics functioned integrally in the ancients' ecstatic contact, for sound offers a spatiality closer to an *absorbtion* within things. He issues a very strong warning that although the experiencing of ecstatic contact may have been suppressed, its determinant force.has not gone away. It cannot be forever displaced "to the individual as the poetic rapture of starry nights." Nor can it be banished from the experience of whole nations. He understood World War I to be a rising up of the desire for ecstatic contact, realized through a "new and unprecedented commingling with the cosmic powers."

> Human multitudes, gases, electrical forces were hurled into the open country, high-frequency currents coursed through the landscape, new constellations rose in the sky, aerial space and ocean depths thundered with propellers, and everywhere sacrificial shafts were dug in Mother Earth.

The atmospheric canopy under which this communion was enacted was a tight fit indeed when compared with the cosmos. It was also enacted under the canopy of a soldier's helmet, where a bullet hole shined like the sun. Or under the canopy of the cranium where "the nights of annihilation" shook the "frame of mankind . . . by a feeling that resembled the bliss of the epileptic."

If he had lived past WWII as well, he would have seen the "commingling with cosmic forces" made manifest in toxic water tables and oceans polluted with Trident submarines; stratospheric carpet bombing of Vietnam and the withering of both land and people by Agent Orange; sending Salvadoran death squads airborne and Latin American monoculture; satellite mono-mediaculture and the tattoo of the space laser. And he would have witnessed the script of this fitful abandon being carved like tablets through the roof of the skull by the global rise of theocrazies, the incessant imperatives of capital and patriarchy, and the disciplining promise of nuclear blitzkrieg.

Benjamin says there are two necessary responses. That the mastery of nature must be transformed into a mastery—"if we are to use this term"—of the relationship between nature and humans. And that this must be undertaken concurrently with political revolution. He understood both within the context of monopoly capital: with the destructiveness of the "imperialist mastery of nature" and with the creativity released by proletarian revolution. Although this can be now extended to all forms of domination, the imperialist haunt that is the U.S. remains paramount.

* * * * * * *

151

The Vietnam War was the backdrop which came to the forefront during the days of Judson Dance Theater. The artistic milieu that valued an unnerving candor of daily life could also promote disclosure of the bountiful complicity that daily acquiescence produced. During an event organized by Jon Hendricks at Judson Church called *Evening of Manipulation/Evening of Destruction* Goldstein performed the poetic composition *death: act or fact of dying* and installed a participatory piece.

> Down in the basement of the church I did something with a speech from Lyndon Johnson called *State of the Nation.* It was a room filled with newspapers and five or six tape recorders. Each one had a large, repeating tape loop with LBJ saying things like: "Thank god for modern American medical science: 79,000 of the 85,000 of our wounded soldiers have been returned to the front." "Are the Vietnamese right about us? No, I think they're wrong." And so forth. The audience could change the speed of the machines, cut up and repaste the sounds together. The whole room changed from speech to just noise: a big low howl.

Opposition in the U.S. was generally conceived from one vantage point only, as a non-complicity with homegrown aggression. There was a diminished ability to side with the liberation of the Vietnamese themselves, because of the distances of geography, experience, culture, nation and nationalism, race and racism.

> I had been involved in anti-Vietnamese War demonstrations. But those were really fantasy. I didn't know what Vietnam was like. I'd seen pictures of it.....

Now that the imperial *cantus firmus* sings its familiar refrain in Central America, the situation of domestic opposition is different. For the ingrown conceit that reduces Central America to "our backyard" reveals in the same breath the existence of neighborly talk over the fence. Similar revelation that there existed in Grenada Black revolutionaries who, heaven forbid, spoke English prompted the programmatic U.S. mythification, destabilization, invasion and occupation. With the first language of the hemisphere and the second language in the U.S. being Spanish, imperial fears fester. Not only are there people speaking for self-determination, there are people who are too capable of listening, too capable of dialogue, comradery and love. U.S. puppet regimes must work on the ventriloquist model—Joe and Charlie McCarthy—but by being closer to the tongue, closer to the war's staging, people can see Administered lips moving.

The dedication of *Vision Tree Fragment* "to the people of El Salvador in their struggle for freedom" is the product of actual dialogue, realized in the context of U.S. activist opposition. In the late 60s after their son Yosha was born, Carol Marcy and Goldstein decided they didn't want to raise him in New York City. Then Goldstein, who had been freelancing in orchestras, was asked to play in the Puerto Rican Symphony Orchestra. "So there he was, three months old, basking in these wonderful warm oceanic waters." A tour of the orchestra took Goldstein through Central America.

> I saw the tremendous extremities of poverty and richness in Central America. In places there were young military police, 18-20 years old, on every street corner with submachine guns. Every corner. In the daytime you'd see very poor people. In the evenings quite different people would drive up in their very rich cars with furs and jewelry to hear Tchaikovsky and Beethoven.

Each stop on the tour would last two or three days. During their stay in San Salvador, the musicians from the orchestra were invited by a group of Salvadoran musicians to a park where they were honored with a marimba concert and feast.

> They had marimbas that were huge. Some were twelve feet long. Some were three feet long. They had an ensemble with four, five or six marimbas and they played a beautiful concert for us. Then they roasted a whole cow on a spit in front of us. Most of the musicians wouldn't eat it, and at this time I was a vegetarian. But I ate it anyway just because. It was tough, horrible. But it was wonderful.

So the dedication of *Vision Tree Fragment* was a return gesture, cemented by an associative link between the wood of the maple limb and the wood of the marimbas. "Yea, that was very simple. They were so wonderful and I was just offering it back to them." This offering was first given in Boston during an event of the Artists Call for Central America. Goldstein had also worked during Artists Call with another person in putting together an exhibition of Nicaraguan posters, which was displayed at the Massachusetts College of Art. He has also centered other compositions around struggles in Central America. *The Violence of Small Sounds* was for Central America as a whole and *The Edges of Sound Within,* which utilized poems by Otto-Renè Castillo, Rosario Murrillo, Pablo Neruda and Josè Luis Villatoro, was composed for Nicaragua.

The *Vision Tree Fragment* dedication itself is intended as a small gesture to draw attention toward the continuing plight in El Salvador. It has no didactic intent nor, with a word such as "people" being so ripe for demagoguery in the U.S., can it have didactic content. Any type of commentary commensurate with socio-political events is extremely difficult in music without words: "Music rescues name as pure sound—but at the cost of severing it from things." (Adorno)[27] This, of course, does not depoliticize the music but it does promote the notion that there are some cultural activities without socio-political content. Goldstein does not find that notion as prevalent in Europe as it is in the United States.

> People in Europe think about things alot more. There's lots of questioning why. Here we just do something. Here there might be a question of why did you write that note, an aesthetic question. But there they would want to understand this in terms of a larger social and political context—they're not separated out.

The dedication in this sense discourages an institutionalization of separation. This could have been more forcefully communicated, however, if the dedication would have contained information about the Salvadoran musicians, or even Artists Call. In this way, the experiential connection could coax the dedication's detachment into becoming an invocation.

Although commentary may not be possible within the music itself, Goldstein sees another purposefulness: that of healing, especially as it arrives from traditions of shamanism. Invocation, instead of dedication, would serve to make this a more palpable experience.

> Although rubbing a lot doesn't seem very meaningful when compared to the brutality taking place in Central America, there is a simple reason. To me, both [*Vision Tree Fragment* and *from Center of Rainbow, Sounding*] are healing songs. Both are songs that are ways of sounding that have to do with offering of healing or resolution.

I would say that the main reason this might not seem very meaningful in relation to the brutality, and why so much culture in general is reduced to gesture, lies in the way the U.S. exiles its true artists, poets and musicians to the margins of society. In contrast, poetry in Central America "has been a *materially decisive* ideological practice"; it has engaged "directly or indirectly very broad sectors of the population, including those elements which constitute, potentially or in fact, the revolutionary vanguard."[28] This has been a key factor in the radical democratization of Nicaragua. It has aided immeasurably in the healing of the country. It's crucial now that the poets, artists and musicians, from around the world and from the U.S., not be squandered anymore in their attempts to heal, across the board, the damage done and the damage being done.

We'll end with a poem by the Sandinista Minister of Culture, Ernesto Cardenal.[29] (Translation by Alegandro Murguìa in *Volcàn*. © 1983 by City Lights Books)

Ecology

In September by San Ubaldo more coyotes were seen.
Soon after the triumph, more lizards
   in the rivers by San Ubaldo
      On highways more rabbits, mountain cats...
The bird population has tripled, they tell us,
   especially that of snipes.
Noisy snipes come down to swim where
      they see water sparkling.
The Somocistas also destroyed lakes, rivers and mountains
   They changed the course of rivers for their ranches.
The Ochomogo dried up last summer.
The Sinecapa dried by ravages of the big landowners.
The Rio Grande of Matagalpa dried up during the war
      over by the Sebaco plains
They built two dams on the Ochomogo,
      and capitalist chemical wastes
spilt into the Ochomogo had the fish swimming
      like drunkards.
      The Boaco River with black waters.
The Moyuá Lagoon dried up. A Somocista colonel
stole lands from *campesinos*
      and built a dam.
The Moyuá Lagoon that for centuries had made
      that site beautiful.
   (But the little fish will return.)
They ravaged and repressed.
      Few iguanas in the sun, few armadillos.
The green Caribbean turtle was sold by Somoza.
Turtle eggs and iguanas were exported by the truckload.
      The Caribbean turtle wiped out.
The saw-fish of the Gran Lago finished off by José Somoza.
The jaguar of the jungle in danger of extinction,
   its soft fur the color of jungle,
and the puma, the tapir in the mountains
(like the *campesinos* in the mountains).
And the poor Chiquito River! Its disgrace
that of the whole nation. Somocismo reflected in its waters.
The Chiquito River of León, fed at the source
by sewers, the wastes of soap factories and tanneries,
white water from soap factories,
                  red from the tanneries;

155

plastics on the river bed, chamber pots, rusted irons. That's
what Somocismo left us.
(We have to see it beautiful and clear again, singing to the sea.)
And into the lake of Managua all the black waters and chemical
    wastes of Managua,
        And over by Solentiname, on the isle of La Zanata
a great white mound stinking
                  with saw-fish skeletons.
But the saw-fish can now breathe
along with fresh water shark.
Tisma is once again full of regal herons
             reflected in its mirrors.

It has many starlings, snipes, guises, widgeons.
    The flora has benefited as well.
The armadillos are very happy with this government.
   We shall reclaim the forests, rivers, lagoons.
We're going to decontaminate the lake of Managua.
Not only humans desired liberation.
The whole ecology wanted it. The revolution
   is also of lakes, rivers, trees, animals.

Notes

Special appreciation goes to the following people for their assistance with this essay. Shira Cion, Dean Kahn, Reese Williams and especially Malcolm Goldstein. Thank you all.

1. Paula Gunn Allen, "The Sacred Hoop: A Contemporary Indian Perspective on American Indian Literature," in Jerome Rothenberg and Diane Rothenberg, eds., *Symposium of the Whole,* University of California, 1983, p. 180.

2. *Vision Soundings,* produced by Malcolm Goldstein (MG 2) 1985. Also *Soundings for Solo Violin* (MG 1) 1980. Available from Malcolm Goldstein, P.O. Box 134, Sheffield, VT 05866. And *The Seasons: Vermont,* Folkways Records (FX 6242) 1983.

3. All quotes, unless otherwise noted, are from a talk we had on 24 May 1986 at his Brookline Village apartment (Boston) or from personal correspondence. Please see Goldstein's "The Politics of Improvisation" in *Perspectives of New Music,* Vol. 21, Nos. 1 & 2 (Fall-Winter 1982/Spring-Summer 1983). "Improvisation: Towards a Whole Musician in a Fragmented Society" in *I.S.A.M. Newsletter* (Institute for Studies in American Music), Volume XII, No. 2 (May 1983). "Improvisation: People Making Music" in catalogue for New Music America Festival, Houston 1986. For a fine discussion of art/politics/nature see Lucy R. Lippard, *Overlay: Contemporary Art and the Art of Prehistory,* New York, 1983.

4. Henry David Thoreau, *Walden, or Life in the Woods,* New York, 1929, p. 306. A plectrum is used to pluck a musical instrument. It's also the spur on a bird's foot or wing. There was a time when the sound was placed indoors, but he didn't bring it: "I also heard the whooping of the ice in the pond, my great bedfellow in that part of Concord, as if it were restless in its bed and would fain turn over—were troubled with flatulency and bad dreams. . ." p. 307.

5. "By materialism we understand above all acknowledgment of the priority of nature over 'mind,' or if you like, the physical level over the biological level, and of the biological level over the socio-economic and cultural level; both in the sense of chronological priority (the very long time which supervened before life appeared on earth, and between the origin of life and the origin of man), and in the sense of conditioning which nature *still* exercises on man and will continue to exercise at least for the foreseeable future." Sebastiano Timpanaro, *On Materialism,* London (1975), cited in Raymond Williams, "Problems of Materialism" in *Problems in Materialism and Culture,* London (1980). See also his "Ideas of Nature" in the same collection.

6. Cited in Walter Benjamin, "Theses on the Philosophy of History" in *Illuminations,* New York, 1969.

7. Following Murray Bookchin's thesis: The very notion of the domination of nature by man stems from the very real domination of human by human. Cf. his *The Ecology of Freedom,* Palo Alto, 1982.

8. Cf. Sally Banes on Judson, *Democracy's Body,* UMI Research Press, 1985. Another statement by Goldstein on Judson from the original transcript of an interview with Grita Insam for the Wiener Festwochen '83 catalogue:

I was very fortunate many years ago, to have participated in the Judson Dance Theater, where I perceived, by working with dancers, the physicality of their moving; but also having them ask me to do certain things: to make certain sounds and to move certain ways, while making sounds. Actually, I have had choreographed pieces of music for me, where I was told not what sound to make, but to make a sound while I jumped or while I was running or leaning over . . . And' that obviously turned me upside down, because when you study music, both in music schools and when you study violin, you don't do things like that. You are learning mostly, not about your body, not about space or anything like that, but about little black notes running around on the page, which you have to realize as specifically as possible.

9. Henry David Thoreau, "Walking" in *The Portable Thoreau,* New York, 1981.

10. Walter J. Ong, *Presence of the Word,* Yale University, 1967, p. 118.

11. William Labov, *Language in the Inner City,* University of Pennsylvania, 1973, and Roger D. Abrahams, *The Man-of-Words in the West Indies,* Johns Hopkins University, 1983.

12. In this respect, Goldstein recommended Edmund Carpenter's wonderful book *Eskimo Realities,* New York (1973), especially the observations on carving. See also Carpenter's comments on Eskimo acoustic space which are also pertinent to this essay.

Carving, like singing isn't a thing. When you feel a song within you, you sing it; when you sense a form emerging from ivory, you release it. . . As the carver holds the unworked ivory lightly in his hand, turning it this way and that, he whispers, "Who are you? Who hides there?" And then: "Ah, seal!" He rarely sets out to carve, say a seal, but picks up the ivory, examines it to find its hidden form and, if that's not immediately apparent, carves aimlessly until he sees it, humming or chanting while he works. Then he brings it out: Seal, hidden, emerges. It was always there: he did not create it, he released it; he helped it step forth.(p. 59)

. . .The carver never attempts to force the ivory into uncharacteristic forms, but responds to the material as it tries to be itself, and thus the carving is continually modified as the ivory has its say. . . . Great Western artists sometimes thought in these terms and even expressed themselves so, but with one difference: They were exceptions in their own culture, independently reaching this attitude only after long experience and contemplation; whereas the Eskimo learn it as a mother tongue and daily give it social voice and expression: parent toward child, husband toward wife. (pp. 62-63)

13. Hugo Ball, *Flight Out of Time,* New York, 1974, p. 71.

14. One explanation of Ball's phoneticism is that it was a social abstraction of the polyglot spoke in the cabaret by its patrons expatriated to Switzerland by WWI.

15. Of interest are some of the characteristics of the exceptions. One where the object of gaze is close to the eyes, thus breaking up the usual segmentation of the visual field, approximating the continuous space of sound. The second where the gaze is fixed on strong radiant sources or upon surfaces directly reflecting radiant sources, e.g., St. Ignatius Loyola staring at a running stream or Jacob Boehme locked onto "burnished pewter dish which reflected the sunshine with great bril-

liance." Here too the radiance of sight approaches the vibrance/vibrations of sound. And a third where visuality is absorbed through the repetitions of the breath, which is not so much about sight as finding a pivot for breath and repetition.

16. "Sound situates people in the middle of actuality and in simultaneity, whereas vision situates people in front of things and in sequentiality." Walter J. Ong, *Presence of the Word,* p. 128. This sequentiality can easily dovetail with the repetitive processes of capitalist technical rationalization and commodification. A music based here threatens to be little more than an anthem to the technocracy.

17. From Grita Insam interview for the Wiener Festwochen '83 catalogue.

18. See the discussion by the French philosopher of music Daniel Charles of the act of getting inside sounds as it relates to transience, memory and to power. He counterposes duration within "Western traditional 'great' music" against the non-metrical new musics of Cage and others. With the music of Cage, et al.,

. . . we do not have to *control* durations, but to listen to them, thus freeing ourselves from the idea that every sound is related to other sounds by (logical) implications or hierarchy or structural lines concerning what precedes or follows; we have *to get inside the sound* and let it have its own duration. (original emphasis) From "New Music: Utopia AND Oblivion," in *Performance in Postmodern Culture,* ed. Michel Nenamou and Charles Caramello, Madison, 1977.

19. See Jacques Attali, *Noise: The Political Economy of Music,* University of Minnesota, 1985.

20. Although this isn't the place for it, a fruitful discussion could be built upon Adorno's comments on Schoenberg in the section "Musical Domination of Nature" in *Philosophy of Modern Music* and the genesis of Reich's music out of the tone row, where he didn't "transpose, invert, or retrograde his rows but that he merely repeated them with rhythmic re-groupings." (See K. Robert Schwarz, "Steve Reich: Music as a Gradual Process" Parts I & II in *Perspectives of New Music,* Fall 1980-Summer 1981 and Fall 1981-Summer 1982, p. 383.) Such a discussion would include Adorno's own idea of "the development of the musical forces of production as men's free disposal over the natural material, as the emancipation of freedom from the natural condition."

21. Comments made in Wim Wenders' film *Chambre 666.*

22. Cited in R. Murray Shafer, *The Tuning of the World,* University of Pennsylvania, Philadelphia (1980), p. 228. Capital was historically able to alloy repetition to the machine because of this bliss.

23. Again, Walter Benjamin on hashish. "The music that meanwhile kept rising and falling, I called the rush switches of jazz. I have forgotten on what grounds I permitted myself to mark the beat with my foot. This is against my education, and it did not happen without inner disputation. There were times when the intensity of acoustic impressions blotted out all others." This is a rare observation for, outside the phonics of speech, Benjamin was not verse with sound, leaving music to one uptight Adorno who was Riddled with the Sphincts. The drug state which set his toe tapping seems to have released him into sound as well. With objects subjected to an acoustic immersion, he was surprised at "How things withstand the gaze!" This should be kept in mind in connection with his well-known idea of *aura,* a concept he first developed with friends while on hashish; the visual connotation of

aura must be tempered with aurality. It should also be remembered that the Turkish puppet chess player "historical materialism"—Maelzel's chess player kept alive by Edgar Allan Poe—who inhabits the first of Benjamin's "Theses on the Philosophy of History," had a hookah in its mouth.

24. Mircea Eliade, "Experiences of the Mystic Light" in *Mephistopheles and the Androgyne*, New York, 1965. Originally appearing as "Significations de la 'lumière intérieure'" in *Eranos-Jahrbuch* XXVI, 1957 (Zurich). See also his *Yoga, Immortality and Freedom*, Paris, 1954 and *Shamanism: Archaic Techniques of Ecstasy*, Princeton University, 1964.

25. Walter Benjamin, "One-Way Street" in *Reflections*, New York, 1979.

26. T. W. Adorno, *Minima Moralia: Reflections from Damaged Life*, London, 1974, pp. 222-223.

27. John Beverley, "Poetry and Revolution in Central America," in *The Year Left: An American Socialist Yearbook,* edited by Mike Davis, Fred Pfeil, Michael Sprinker, New York, 1985.

28. *Volcàn,* edited by Alegandro Murguìa and Barbara Paschke for the Roque Dalton Cultural Brigade, City Lights Books, San Francisco, 1983. © 1983 by City Lights Books. With kind permission from City Lights Books; Lawrence Ferlinghetti and Nancy J. Peters, editors. 261 Columbus Avenue, San Francisco, California 94133.

Reese Williams

The space where laughter accumulates holds in reserve for the hot moments of birth and death. Mothers know that a child born in this space will be different from other children, will appear to be lost, will never obey the money culture. A man who chooses to die here knows that he will meet every human who has ever lived. The space is first recognized only as a constant tone, but this sound teaches attention and gradually one begins to hear spirals of individual laughter. Each laugh once recognized takes off again into the larger whirling, a warm and gentle wind. As attention grows stronger, human life slowly dissolves until all that remains is the shared heat.

✻

Her laugh begins in an earlier time, mischieviously breaks through the surface of daily life and swoops away, iridescent green, into the sky of the next world. Back again in a flash of lightning, it is the advance sounding of her desire, her need to continually find new ways of touching Earth.

His laugh is still moving long after it has ceased to sound, so powerful were the initial bursts. Like water flowing into an open meadow, it spreads smoothly across the ground, enveloping each shape, entering every opening.

The two sounds, heard together, become a young child painting on a white wall. X's in blue, then red. Spirals like giant fingerprints and a yellow ball for the Sun. The paint drips to make geese, snakes, and upside down monkeys which lead the way to the multi-armed lobster man, his twelve arms spinning backwards as he runs silently onward.

*

Out the door and immediately the boy is running, running for pleasure — no other reason. He always runs the brick path which leads from the front door around the side of the house — something irresistible in the curve. He leans his body into it and pumps his legs as fast as he can.

Just past the turn the path ends, and without breaking stride he leaps two steps down onto the grass. Eyes on the ground, arms and legs at full speed, he heads into the next turn. At the corner there is a step up as the grass changes to concrete patio — this is the one hard part. But once past this corner, he can sprint down the straightaway, a few seconds of crazed blood charge before he has to remember why he came out of the house.

He makes the turn and begins this last surge, gradually shifting his eyes back up to the horizon. Suddenly, from the opposite direction, running straight toward him, a large stag deer with full antlers. The sound of hoofs clacking and scraping on the concrete, and the dry squealing of tennis shoes, as the two skid to stop just before crashing into each other. An instant of utter confusion, deer and boy nose to nose: the solid black eyes of the deer so wide apart, and the white hands of the boy, frozen in a stopping gesture. With one glance the line breaks, and time comes spilling in from all directions. They have a thousand new lives to choose from, but each one knows, knows from instinct, that what has come through the opening is not to be used. Simultaneously their bodies lower to the right following the eyes, muscles tense then explode, and they are running again.

*

House on fire, rooms collapsing from bursts of heat. Coming from the orange-red is the sound of grinding steel. It is wartime: his father is dead, flat out, mouth gaping, and his mother is on the far side of the river, mute.

A squad of frogmen swimming upstream in the rushing water. Multi-armed and without faces, black rubber completely covering their bodies, they swim like robots straight toward him. Naked and alone, his life blows apart into three satellites, drifting silently in the dark sky. Each satellite has a screen showing a different part of his life, but there is nothing he can do to put things back together.

They crash land in the desert, metal fuselage scrapping rock and sand. Emergency doors explode off and he slides down a ramp to the ground. Walking away from the wreckage into the night, the new death begins to unloosen the pain of the earlier one. He lies down on the ground and his body folds and refolds itself, taking one shape after another. A coyote comes in close to investigate, holding his head low to the ground, listening intently to the snapping sounds. One by one each bone in the man's body is breaking. His cells are at war with each other and they fight all through the night. Just before dawn the battle ends. His body comes to rest in the spiral form of an ear, and he is waiting silently with the others, listening for the arrival of the Sun.

*

171

A constant tone. Always the same, but I hear it differently with each new day. Inside, a wandering constellation of the perfected cries of man and animal.

Periodically the tone goes jagged, like that of a helicopter, as one human takes another high up into the sky and pushes him out the door, bound and gagged, toward the ocean far below.

Spinning down and down, the man climbs the mountain of terror. When he reaches the highest pinnacle, a twinge of sadness radiates out across the surface of Earth (as it always does whenever anyone masters this great summit). He raises his right hand to the sky, then he leaps off. Energy long saved for this moment ignites his spinal column, flushing out every cell in his body. All that was in the mind is driven out the mouth in one long piercing scream. Thousands of filaments rise up into the dome of the skull and instantly re-form the life. What once came with the seed now leaves through the fontanel.

Swirling blue and white. . . Closer, it is water, the ocean. And in the water, millions of silver jets — each of his cells now a salmon. They are returning, each with the same desire, into the mouth of the river. Leaping and thrusting in the white water, free within instinct, relentless toward union.

*

Slowly, one to one, we are coming to meet each other. It's not the impossible task the governments make it appear to be.

You know when you have connected with someone by the feeling, a swirling phosphorescence up and down the spine.

Speech is not so important, the exchange happens in a different way. Heat generated from the meeting goes to nourish the brain which is evolving a new area, a thin layer which will wrap around the existing brain, a thin layer which will carry human life beyond the atomic war era.

*

Before taking off into the sky, she extends the curve of her yellow neck to the Sun and screeches, *O-aah O-aah*. For a few moments, with her wings fully spread, she repeats this sound, and with each inhale she moves closer to flight. One last screech, this one as if there will never be the chance for another, and she strains her body up from the ground, flapping her wings as fast as she can.

Soaring away from the dense sound of the island colony, she grows alone with one overpowering desire. Below, the ocean water is clear. Underneath the surface, the pulsing form of a school of silver herring. Letting the wind shape her circle, she enters into an orbit above the fish. Her wings wave in a slow rhythm, then glide, then move again, all the while her head holding steady, eyes focused in one beam. With each orbit, she comes nearer to the vibration of the fish. At the base of her skull, brain cells, one by one, lock on to their telepathic pulse.

Like a huge serpent, the school of fish undulating in slow curves. One curve comes up into the warm water right at the surface. Suddenly, a flash of light reflecting off the silver. This is the signal. The Sun has marked one fish for her, and immediately she is diving. Plunging straight down, her eyes fixed on the one point, she bursts into the water, re-surfacing an instant later with the fish throbbing in her mouth.

*

Middle afternoon, the Jaguarundi lies crouched on a narrow concrete ledge next to the plate glass window that separates him from the viewers. He is quiet, ready to receive what will come forth.

I bring my head down close to his, into his magnetic field and suddenly we are resonating, two points of heat in a falling white. He is immensely sad, a boundless landscape. . . and I feel more alone than ever before. Inside his sadness, woven across the dominant, is a more subtle rhythm. It is a courage. Not the one humans can imagine, but something closer to plant life — the knowledge to wait, the freedom to hold balance in each given situation.

It is very hot today, over a hundred degrees. This cat is away from his grassland home forever, imprisoned in a recreation zone. Like all cats he can only cool himself through his mouth. With eyes closed and tongue protruding just slightly, his diaphragm moves in a fast shallow rhythm, allowing the rest of his body to relax into a slow death.

*

End of a day, this one on a high desert mesa. I walk away from the highway for a half a mile or so into the scrub desert and sit in the clay soil to watch the sunset. A flat empty landscape dominated by the clear blue sky. Usually I experience the Sun as a brilliant object, but today I see it as an opening.

I am tired, and as the Sun disappears my eyes slowly close. When they open again, a black dog is sitting directly in front of me. His lips are pulled back, exposing his teeth, and his body is quivering. One paw is slightly raised and he is leaning forward, almost to the point of falling. After a moment I understand that what I am seeing is a very intense smiling, one that is growing stronger and stronger. After another moment I know that this dog is the happiest living creature I have ever seen. All I can do is return his smile. At first I am self-conscious, but as my face slowly widens and the teeth become visible, his body begins to shake in pleasure, collapsing down to the ground. Then, digging his paws into the clay soil, he slides over to touch.

*

Inside the trunk of a pine, water slowly rising. Outside, diving water, off the edge of the cliff toward rocks far below.

For a hundred years and more this tree will breathe the falling white sound, silently rooted in his duty to make water well up from the earth and into the sky.

A lower branch points directly to me inviting one more human to listen. My ears become fish in the trance of water, white changes to blue-green and I am drenched with the sound of her voice rising to the high note.

*

. . . there is a supreme Self which is the inhabitant or soul of the universe. All we know is that it has a voice like a woman, a voice so fine and gentle that even children cannot become afraid. What it says is: 'be not afraid of the universe.'

Najagneq, the Eskimo shaman, as told to Rasmussen.

May Stevens

A God Among the Taxicabs

A leaf from Ithaca

I sent you a leaf   a fall leaf   it said
You are radiant   you are red   as the hart
upon the mountain   as a god among the
taxicabs   Did you hear what the leaf said?

Some people died who never died before she said
They died just now she said reading the *Times*
Her skin was pink   Her flesh concealed the bones
inside   She pretended she was a chair
hoping death would flash past   Sat still as a sofa
A dress laid over   Two shoes neatly placed

When I come after six months   a year   she waves
Moving from chair to bed to table she opens the
door to the field   waits to receive words of praise
and affection   The days of no figure crossing the
field have moved to this moment   We are together
We drive off   She has nothing to say   She is humming

Into the earphone   flustered   Good morning Good morning
and a pause to right the phone   I am deeply consoled
by the life in her voice   We discuss arthritis
and ointments   I profess my love   do rituals of
ending to hang the phone on   The phone clicks
before my final variation   But I think when she
walks back to her chair by the kitchen door   next to the TV
when she hangs her cane on the chair post and sits down
in her usual place   heads are still turned   and she sits in
a buzz of contentment
The postcard says: Everybody knows me

In the night she wakes and wanders
about the room   One hand held up
the other fends the unknown shapes
What is this place?   I find her glasses
light the lamp   identify myself
Is that where you sleep?   I take her
to my bed and lie   one arm across
her body as I did forty years ago
telling her that I will never leave
her   lying as I do now that I can
take her pain away   rub out the fear
for more than these few unmoored
hours before I take her back

We are two women under a rod of light
The glasses have paper bags on them and
the toilet is sealed   The mirrors show
we are old, one older than the other and
related by years of words and postcards
There are no other ways but these

We meet in this or another room We eat
We sleep   We talk a little   We spend
two days   And then you ask is it you
who calls on the phone with the same name?

We slide the glass doors open   Freshness
floods the room   We pull two chairs to
face the rain and sit wrapped in a great
blanket

Loosened strands slip down deep divided back
Buttocks' shelf slides to creasing thighs Knees
keep a partial crouch   Belly slings body center
forward over a hairless pouch   She lifts each breast
soaping the smell of age   She (matter self-propelled
mushrooms pink and lavender, lustful, greedy, feeding)
steps into air, hands stroking space, trusting someone
is there to towel her dry, pin remnant hair, give back
her name, her watch, her story   She loves being clean
but who has time to wash her every day? Is she a baby
with a future? She loves hair dressed but fears over-
handling may make it thin   Dampish still, flushed
talced, her body blooming, she swings foot, hums
nightgowned beside the bed, waits for milk and pills
Glasses folded under pillow, sheet clutched high
one hand slipped between her thighs, she sleeps a
sleep she will deny, in tongues converses with
familiars, unshareable   No she did not speak she lies
keeping her secret garden, loving the long continuous
dialog, absorbing, obsessing, warm and sweet as ex-
crement newly made, unspeakable, but hers, and real

Class

My mother likes to dress up. When pleased with an elegant new outfit, mine or hers, she exclaims, "Some class." Class, to my mother, is an aspiration. She doesn't see anything wrong with lifting herself out of the commonplace to a look that shows the taste (education) and the leisure to dress with care. She knows that my father liked her better and would have liked me better when/if we got ourselves up in such a way as to show we wanted to please him and others who looked on us, not sexually as women, but in a class sense as women who respected ourselves, our neighbors, and the man who earned a living for us.

He wanted to be proud. He worked hard (sloughed off only to the extent that was conventional, permitted, in fact required by his co-workers) for his wages and used them for his own comfort and ours, to enhance his own standing in the community and ours. His sending me to college was the same kind of decision that rising in class was worth spending money on. He didn't expect, of course, that college would make me dress badly (jeans and shirts and long hair) even years after I graduated. Nor behave badly either (radical politics, peace marches, signing petitions and other intemperate behavior). He never imagined that lifting me out of his class would produce in me an allegiance to his class that *he* did not feel. He had swallowed the dream. But it's more than a dream because the books and the art that raise you from one class to another, to bourgeois life, are indeed capable of providing a better life—and also the means of critiquing that life.

Class aspiration never meant money to my mother nor to me. It did not mean household help, nor fur coats, nor holidays. It meant looking good (well-dressed, well-coiffed), like the minister's wife or Mrs. Lovejoy's daughter—the women who took pains with these things. I think that was what we admired most. People who did things with care and taste. Men who kept their cars shiny, women who kept their houses spotless, whose children showed that care had gone into their training. Men and women who raised flowers, mowed lawns; women who set a pretty table and placed a crocheted doily on the back and armrests of the upholstered chairs.

My mother ironed my dresses to starchy crispness. My favorite teacher touched my pleated blouse and said, "Your mother must love you very much." Even now nothing pleases my mother like my fluffing her hair, pinning earrings to her soft old lobes, covering the wrinkled skin that hangs in folds about her neck and arms and thighs with fresh cloth and neat lapels. We tell her she looks like a college professor.

It's simple   I am my baby's swaddling
lifeliness torn and dangling   My breast hangs
to the bed   snuffles among folds   blind
dependent   pokes towards its sheath   your mouth

Your stone gums suck my titty   gone hard
caked   the milk waits   dries
no trickle   only the dry crack
in the heart of things   Your dry mouth
my dry nipple   a match   a pair
a simple fit   There's nothing to it   When your mouth
was succulent and primed me all day long
I thought we would never come apart

I carry you now in my head
connected to all my systems
as once you swung in the womb
I rock you there in my brain
foaming in fluids, sloshed in nutrient dreams,
I feel you kicking   The membrane thins
It opens   You spill out   I weep you

The womb is a limb
It's a handle, a prop
a tool that speaks   It feels
the fat pads on your small hand
the place on your shoulder my head could reach
your eyes, my eyes returned to me
The womb is a limb, a handle, a prop
a tool that speaks   Mine listens:
it hears your bright hallooo

You're almost 90 I say
She laughs
That's pretty old I say
Does it hurt I say
How does it feel to be old?
What is it like?
She searches patient with me
It's the way it is
She says   and I know how
Simplicity and wisdom are the same,
          the circle coming back on itself   Neruda:
The blood of the children in the streets is like
          the blood of the children in the streets.
My life is not like   it is unlike   why pretend?
There are no mistakes   only choices   I want to get
to the bottom of things: how can I care about things
          when he took our life?
For he made fish hide and crabs scuttle   the sun
shine on his skin   seals laugh   puppy dogs roll over
his father and I gasp at the splashing brightness
          of his arrogant life
The blood of my child is mixed with earth
          his ash on water; the things he liked
          go on   past his liking
          How can they do that?

You read our names You kiss the image of you and me laughing
You're famous I say You laugh at the end of your 89 years
your mouth like the beak of a young bird curling out of the
concave dark of this summer day at the end of your valid life

Mother, I'll go with you

through all the advent days

to see that all the lamps of love

shoot out their undimmed rays

You laugh at our picture You kiss it, for fondness, you say
Haltingly you read to me   I write your name

You can go

I hug you close   Take care of your ribs
Keep your arms in their hollows   Don't talk
The milk that is spilled
              in the well of your neck
I will write white words with it
            if you'll be still
Unfold   the layers of your skin
that let out a limb   Make a pact with
brittle or pliant   Under the blanket
ends of the ribs   north of the saddle bone
      up on the blanket   sponge of your veins
chips of your fingers   float like a shell
      sea's tissue to sea's stone
         End formally

Hold up your head on its hawkcords
Hood with your eyes the dark you see
ahead of me   Scratch your nose a little
Tuck in your mouth over the drowsy gullet
Suck in the places your skin falls to dream
      under the jutting bone
        There is great beauty

Drink milk
   Color comes to the lips
      You thrum when I hug you and squeeze you
      as if you were my newborn daughter
Brush with your hand
the back of my hand
with faint desire

Don't eat   Turn your head to the wall
Nothing has flavor: cold paste on a sharp
edged spoon   Not for you   No   You've decided
Serenely you smile   in control of your life
You're safe   deep inside   Curl up in your cot
strapped to its sides   Nothing can happen
You are washed   changed   pulled from slumber
    for riddles   you have no time for
Close down your eyes   Soon I'll be gone
Clamp shut your ears and jaw   Find your way
    to the smallest light
Enter so softly
    it's not an event
        I won't even know

Theresa Hak Kyung Cha

POLYMNIA   SACRED POETRY

(The ninth, and last, section of *Dictee*, Tanam Press, 1982)

She remembered that she had once drank from this well. A young woman was dipping into the well all alone and filling two large jars that stood beside her. She remembered that she had walked very far. It had been a good distance to the village well. It was summer. The sun became brighter at an earlier hour, the temperature soaring quickly, almost at once.

Her mother had given her a white kerchief to wear on her head to avoid the strong rays and a lightly woven smock which was also white.

The heat rises from the earth, diminishing the clear delineations of the road. The dust haze lingers between earth and sky and forms an opaque screen. The landscape exists inside the screen. On the other side of it and beyond.

From a distance the figure outlines the movement, its economy, without extraneous motion from the well to the jar. The repetition of lowering the bucket into the well, an adept gesture that comes to her without a thought given to it, she performs it with precision and speed.

She too was wearing a white kerchief around her thick black hair braided in a single knot down to her back, which swung forward when she leaned against the well. She wore an apron over the skirt which she had gathered and tied to keep it from the water.

Approaching the well, the sound becomes audible. The wooden bucket hitting the sides echoes inside the well before it falls into the water. Earth is hollow. Beneath.

She did not look up at the young girl standing still before her. She saw her walking towards the well in slow paces, holding in her left hand, a small white bundle. Upon reaching the well she stopped still, no longer forced to pursue her pace. She opened her mouth as if to speak, then without a word, searched for a shaded area and sat down.

The proximity of the well seemed to cool her. She exhaled a long sigh. She closed her eyes briefly. The dust and heat had swelled inside them and she could not clearly focus her vision. When she opened her eyes, she could see the tiny pools of spilled water on the rocks surrounding the well and the light reflecting in them.

The second jar was almost full. She heard faintly the young girl uttering a sequence of words, and interspersed between them, equal duration of pauses. Her mouth is left open at the last word. She does not seem to realize that she had spoken.

She looked at the stone well, as the woman drew in the bucket. She followed each movement with her eyes. The woman rested the bucket on the rim of the well and reached inside her apron bringing out a small porcelain bowl. The chipped marks on it were stained with age, and there ran a vein towards the foot of the bowl where it was beginning to crack. She dipped the bowl into the bucket and filled it to the brim. She handed it to the child to drink.

She drinks quickly the liquid. Earth is cooler as it descends beneath. She looked up at the woman. Her eyes became clearer. She saw that the woman was smiling. Her brow fell softly into an arc on each side of her temples. Her eyes were dark and they seemed to glow from inside the darkness.

The child smiled back to her timidly from her seat. Her arms hugged her knees and her small palms wrapped perfectly the roundness of the bowl. The young woman asked her what she was doing so far away from home. The child answered simply that she was on her way home from the neighboring village to take back remedies for her mother who was very ill. She had been walking from daybreak and although she did not want to stop, she was very tired and thirsty, so she had come to the well.

The woman listened and when the child finished her story, she nodded and gently patted the child's head. She then brought over a basket and sat down beside her. The basket was filled with many pockets and she began to bring out one by one each pocket drawn with a black string. She said that these were special remedies for her mother and that she was to take them to her. She gave her instructions on how to prepare them.

She took off the kerchief that she wore and placed it on her lap. She took the bowl and said she must serve the medicines inside the bowl. After she had completed her instructions, she was to keep the tenth pocket and the bowl for herself as a gift from her. She placed the white bowl in the center of the white cloth. The light renders each whiteness iridescent, encircling the bowl a purple hue. She laid all the pockets inside the bowl, then, taking the two diagonal corners of the cloth, tied two knots at the center and made a small bundle.

She gives the bundle to the child to hold in her right hand and says for her to go home quickly, make no stops and remember all she had told her. The child thanks her and stands. She gives her a deep bow.

She began walking very rapidly. Her steps seemed to move lighter than before. After a while she turned around to wave to the young woman at the well. She had already left the well. She turned and looked in all directions but she was not anywhere to be seen. She remembered her words about stopping on her way and she started to run.

Already the sun was in the west and she saw her village coming into view. As she came nearer to the house she became aware of the weight of the bundles and the warmth in her palms where she had held them. Through the paper screen door, dusk had entered and the shadow of a small candle was flickering.

Tai-Chi	First, the universe.
Leung Yee	Second, Ying and Yang.
Sam Choy	Third, Heaven, Earth and Humans.
Say Cheung	Fourth, the Cardinals, North South, East, West.
Ng Hang	Fifth, the five elements, Metal Wood, Water, Fire, Earth.
Lok Hop	Sixth, Four cardinals and the Zenith and Nadir.
Chut Sing	Seventh, the seven stars, the Big Dipper
Bat Gwa	Eight, the Eight Diagrams.
Gow Gee Lin Wan	Ninth, Unending series of nines, or nine points linked together.
Chung Wai	Tenth, a circle within a circle a series of concentric circles.

Tenth, a circle within a circle, a series of concentric circles.

Words cast each by each to weather
avowed indisputably, to time.
If it should impress, make fossil trace of word,
residue of word, stand as a ruin stands,
simply, as mark
having relinquished itself to time to distance

Lift me up mom to the window the child looking above too high above her view the glass between some image a blur now darks and greys mere shadows lingering above her vision her head tilted back as far as it can go. Lift me up to the window the white frame and the glass between, early dusk or dawn when light is muted, lines yield to shades, houses cast shadow pools in the passing light. Brief. All briefly towards night. The ruelle is an endless path turning the corner behind the last house. Walls hives of stone by hand each by each harbor the gold and reflect the white of the rays. There is no one inside the pane and the glass between. Trees adhere to silence in attendance to the view to come. If to occur. In vigilence of lifting the immobile silence. Lift me to the window to the picture image unleash the ropes tied to weights of stones first the ropes then its scraping on wood to break stillness as the bells fall peal follow the sound of ropes holding weight scraping on wood to break stillness bells fall a peal to sky.

The word *tanam* is related to the Sanskrit *Anantam twam*
meaning "endless, thou." The "endlessness" reflects in a way
of reciting chant which involves the breaking up of a text
into syllables and the continuous reordering of them in all
combinations, both as a means of obtaining mastery over the
sound system of the chant and of acquiring insight into
the truth within the text. There is a point where movement
ceases, where sound returns to Silence, where the active
individual melts into the great tradition.

Design by Reese Williams
Printed by Thomson-Shore, Inc.

Thanks to Paul Arkava, Phil Mariani and
Joni Mitchell for help with production.